DAD can't KNOW

Xo,
Eva Marks

EVA MARKS

Copyright © 2023 by Eva Marks

All rights reserved.

No part of this publication may be reproduced, distributed, or transmitted in any form or by any means, including photocopying, recording, or other electronic or mechanical methods, without the prior written permission of the publisher, except as permitted by U.S. copyright law. For permission requests, contact authorevamarks@gmail.com

The story, all names, characters, and incidents portrayed in this production are fictitious. No identification with actual persons (living or deceased), places, buildings, and products is intended or should be inferred.

Book Cover by Eva Marks

A Note from the Author

Dad Can't Know is a steamy, taboo novella, containing explicit and graphic scenes and kinks intended for mature audiences only.

Trigger and Content Warnings

Dad's best friend, ASMR kink, age gap, praise, dirty talking alpha, sexual harassment (not by the hero), touch her and die, neglecting mother of the heroine.

About the Book

No one *plans* to fall for their dad's best friend. But I did...

Callum Reinhart moved across the country two years ago. I was *finally* just over 18 when he left and cut ties with us, taking away with him the opportunity to tell him how I'd stopped thinking of him as Uncle Callum and started thinking of him as an older, wiser, sexy man.

But he's back now, two years later, and so much has changed.

My mom abandoned us. My dad is an emotional mess.

And Callum doesn't look at me like I'm a kid anymore.

He's as hungry for me as I am for him. We know it's forbidden—dirty and intense.

That's not enough to stop us, though. Even though we should.

Not when it feels so good.

All I can do now is keep it a secret as best I can, because there's one thing I know for certain: my dad can *never* know...

PROLOGUE
Robin

Two months earlier

"Dad?" I call out, slamming the door to my parents' penthouse behind me. "Mom?"

There's an eerie silence in the foyer of my childhood home in New York's Upper West Side, interrupted only by the vehement thrashing of my heart. If I *felt* something wasn't right on the way over, now I'm sure of it.

I don't bother kicking off my biker boots like Mom orders us to do. Fuck that, manners are the last thing on my mind, as is the predictive analytics elective course that I've been waiting for these past two and a half years in college.

Eva Marks

My younger sister, Adele, texted me to go check on him and Mom because neither have answered their phones since this morning. Haven't checked their messages, either, which never happens.

These people are glued to their phones harder than Jack clung to the damn door in *Titanic*.

Dad is on it nonstop for his work as the owner of a Wall Street hedge fund managing firm; either he answers emails or goes over the news and latest trends. And Mom, while she doesn't have a job, claims her girlfriends and their gossip keep her busier than Dad.

They're always on it, and they always answer.

Nothing and no one else matters at the moment, except for them.

My boots thump against the sickeningly clean marble floors as I storm into the expansive living room on the first floor.

Expansive and empty.

Considering either of them could be inside the soundproof kitchen Mom had barricaded some years ago, I jog over there. I push through the whitewashed, heavy wooden doors to get in, switching on the light and looking in.

The white marble breakfast island where I can usually find Dad reading the latest finance news is empty. Mom isn't at the fridge getting her bottle of Chardonnay.

Similarly, to the living room, the kitchen is also empty.

I run back out, calling them through the panic that clings to my every pore.

"Mom!" My shout bangs on the walls, goes off the floor-to-ceiling windows overlooking the city, and rounds back to my tightly wound chest.

It hurts, but I don't falter.

"Dad!" I shout again, then curse under my breath, "Goddammit, Adele."

I'm not resenting my sister for being away. I wholeheartedly supported her to enroll in the college of her dreams in New Jersey, where she started studying this year. She wanted to be like me, to embrace her independence, and I was her number one fan.

Still am. I just hate that she's not around today. I could really use someone here with me to tell me nothing horrible waits for me at the top of the stairs.

In my panic, my brain concocts the worst-case scenario. My parents aren't criminals or associated with that kind of people—not that I know of. They are, however, wealthy, and influential. They do appear on magazine covers. They might have been targeted.

The fact that the alarm hadn't been disabled when I walked in doesn't guarantee the house wasn't broken into. All it takes is someone savvy enough to hack the system, and *poof!* you're inside the house.

A shaky breath escapes past my lips. I don't want to find them hurt, or worse, find a ransom note on their pillow.

Terror creeps up my spine, my insides spinning and turning. I'm not easily fazed by anything, but I'm sure the thought of being an orphan at the age of twenty would fuck with anyone's psyche.

I climb up one stair. The railing dents the flesh on my fingers from holding it so tight.

"D-Dad?" I go up another stair. The more the terrorizing pictures filter into my head, the lower my voice drops. "Mom?"

Two of the longest seconds of my life pass until I hear him. "Up here, Robi."

Dad.

A stupid, relieved sob contorts my entire face.

Fuck, since when have I turned into such a fucking hysterical softy?

"It's me." The stairs disappear behind me as I eat them two at a time. At the landing, I yank my phone out of my jeans pocket, shooting Adele a text to tell her our parents are fine.

He is, isn't he? I mean, he answered. He has to be fine.

On trembling feet, I cross the hallway down to their bedroom. There has to be some logical explanation for them going off the grid.

They probably had their much-needed adult alone time. They haven't had any in years. And now, Dad must have gone to put on his robe before he called me up, and he's sitting there watching TV while Mom's in the shower.

Good on them for "phones off" day.

Wish they would've given either my sister or me a head's up, but hey, they're alive and not kidnapped. I prefer this alternative to the other crazy ones.

The door to their room is open, and I peek inside it.

There's a sob.

This time, it isn't mine.

My father sits on the edge of his bed. His elbows rest on his knees, his head is dumped into his palms, and his shoulders shake. Tears leak out to his cheeks. His breaths are loud as if it costs him to inhale.

The man who manages billions of dollars without batting an eye, the father who at forty-three still looks like a strong thirty-year-old with his head full of blond hair and lean physique—he cries.

My father doesn't cry.

And me? I'm a powerful, fierce woman at my intern job. I'm a force to be reckoned with at school.

Faced with my sobbing father, though? I'm a fucking mess.

I have no idea how to handle it.

Calling Adele for advice is out of the question. Two years younger than me, an eighteen-year-old, she shouldn't carry this burden, especially while being miles away from us. If I'm losing it, you bet your ass Adele would be borderline hysterical.

No. Not her. I pace silently toward the end of the hallway, tiptoeing into my sister's old room. It takes me a couple of tries, but eventually, I press my thumb to unlock my phone to scroll through my contacts.

Friends and coworkers are an immediate no, too. Dad's business relies on him being composed and in control, and I won't endanger his reputation by spreading out the word that he's breaking down for whatever reason.

There's only one person I can trust, one family friend who would give his life for Dad and vice versa.

Callum Reinhart. Dad's best friend since preschool.

A new kind of dread slithers beneath my skin. He doesn't scare me; that's not it. Unlike most people who fear the presence of the senior partner of a criminal law firm and his interrogative glares, Callum hasn't intimidated me a day in his life.

It's much, much worse than that. A few months before my eighteenth birthday, something changed in the way I saw him. I stopped referring to him as "Uncle Callum" in my head and started looking at him as a man.

A tall, broad-shouldered, steel-blue-eyed *man*. And don't get me started on the new gray streaks in his short brown hair, or how his cologne hits me differently nowadays.

He's not Uncle Callum anymore, at all. Almost a stranger. Except he isn't. This one man I know way, way too well.

And I've done everything in my power to annihilate this desire for him. I stopped calling him for school advice, haven't sent him funny memes—not once in the past two years. The dampness between my thighs whenever he visited us from L.A. provided a powerful motivator for me to do just that.

I can't be rude to him the few times a year he comes to visit. I talk to him. Sit next to him. Listen to him. And I love it; every living cell in my body loves his presence.

But that's it. Staying away from him has been the best alternative for everyone involved.

At least, it has been. Now, it seems like I don't have much of a choice, do I?

Someone needs to help me in order for me to help Dad. If Mom couldn't help him and she might be there in the bathroom, crying instead of taking a shower, there's literally no one else to be here for us.

Call him. He's a man. Just a man. Your Uncle Callum.

Without sparing myself another moment to overanalyze this awkwardness, I click on his contact.

His phone rings once, twice. "Robin?"

Even out of breath during what must be his morning jog, Callum's voice is the warm blanket I need. It shields me from the last horrible ten minutes, in a world where there's only us.

Hey, idiot, your dad's crying in the other room and your mom's MIA. Remember them?

"Yeah, Callum, it's me," I whisper, placing my palm over my lips. To ensure Dad doesn't hear me completely helpless on top of whatever shit he's going through, I back up to the deepest corner of the room. "I-I need your help."

"What happened? Are you all right?" His breathing slows, and the pounding of his sneakers ceases.

"I'm fine."

I'm not.

"Wes—sorry, Dad okay?"

If there was anything to emphasize my inappropriate thoughts and throw me into the present moment, it's this.

"He's crying. He's crying and Adele is in Jersey and Mom's… I can't find her." My words flow out, wrapped up in anxiety and the relief of having someone besides me here. There's no stopping this rambling train. "I don't know what to do, Callum, I can't call anyone, and I… Please, help me."

"Deep breaths, Robin."

He waits, and I do.

"Listen to my voice. Breathe in, breathe out."

In, out.

I rub my chest as the pressure eases off it. "Thank you."

"I didn't do anything," he continues before I get a chance to tell him he did a whole fucking lot. "I have no idea what's going on, and it'll take hours for me to get to you guys. Your dad needs you to pull it together, okay?"

"Okay." I nod to myself.

"Approach it like you do a coding problem; don't think about him as your father." The serenity in his voice engulfs me, promising me everything will be just fine. "Go over to him, hug him. He might tell you what happened, he might not, and that's okay too. So long as you're there."

More air seeps into my lungs. Callum's rugged, running voice soothes me into a state where I'm no longer a weak little girl. Under his instructions, I'm somehow a woman. The want for him resurfaces in the form of heaviness between my thighs, and not without effort, I shove it down to where it belongs—hell for neglectful daughters.

"Okay."

"Go to him," he says. "I'll have my phone on, waiting for you. Call or text me later."

"I will." I push myself off the corner I've been hiding in, empowered by his words. "Thanks, Un—Callum."

"Thank me when we figure out it was just some big misunderstanding. Now, go."

He ends the call.

I don't walk anymore when I go to Dad. I sprint.

"Dad? What happened? Where's Mom?"

My knees hit the rug at his feet. It doesn't hurt me. Doesn't even register when my father, sitting and weeping silent tears in one of his work suits, is suffering.

He clears his throat, lifting his head. I rest a comforting palm on his knee, forcing a smile and looking back into the gray eyes I inherited from him. For the longest moment, he doesn't say anything, barely even blinking. His eyes dance all over the room, then at my feet.

"Your boots, you haven't taken them off. You know your mothe—" Heaviness coats his voice anew, forcing his gaze to turn away to the window. "I guess it doesn't matter anymore, does it?"

DAD can't KNOW

"Is Mom okay?" It's the best I can elucidate, the most I can say.

My throat is so clogged by a myriad of emotions and questions that even these three words are a hardship. But then I remember Callum's words, and I treat it like a coding problem. I've faced work deadlines, grueling exams, a couple of almost-crashes on my motorcycle. I can and I will do it.

Because this isn't about me. It's about my parents. The two people who brought me into this world, who love me fiercely, who applaud me and pick me up whenever I fall.

They have to be okay. And if not, I have to be okay for them.

"Dad?"

"Your mother is fine," he says to the window, talking to the snowflakes falling outside this January night.

It's a full-blown winter in New York, though judging the sweat forming on my forehead you would've believed we're well into July. "What is it? I'm freaking out, Dad."

"She's fine,"—he sucks in a sharp breath—"with another man."

I open my lips to start a sentence. A question. A scream to reach through the noise-proof walls of the building and into our neighbors' apartments—hell, even to the street.

Eva Marks

What comes out is a feeble, "What?"

"Yeah." He scratches the back of his neck, twisting his head to me. "She... Brody, her ex from... from fucking high school, he messaged her about a year ago. Apparently... Goddammit."

Lead sinks to the pit of my stomach. I mentally scrub it off.

I'm not breaking down today.

I move to sit next to him on the bed, placing an arm around him and resting my head on his shoulder. He offered me a million comforting hugs over the years, and it breaks my heart to have us switch.

It encourages him to speak.

"She wasn't over him, your mother. Twenty-three years of marriage and two beautiful children weren't enough to take him off her mind. *I* wasn't enough." His voice cracks at the end.

"You are. You're the best dad, the best husband ever. It's just a misunderstanding, I'm sure of it." I reiterate Callum's logic.

"It's not." Dad pats my shoulder, sitting up straighter. On his other side, he grabs a pale-cream folder, holding it out to me.

The lead in my stomach dips deeper, sinking my lungs with it. I don't need to see what's in it to guess what's inside. "Divorce papers?"

"Yes." His sigh is defeated as he tosses them to the rug. The white papers fall out, landing in a heap of black letters on white paper. So simple, yet so life-altering all at once.

"It'll be okay, Dad," I lie.

Dad, whose honesty is a part of his DNA, doesn't. "Not for a while, Robi." He pats my knee. "We'll get through it, someday. As a family. We will."

His broken smile slashes my resolve to be strong.

Your dad needs you to pull it together.

I play Callum's words in my head, drawing out of me that extra bit of strength I've been searching for. It forges me into something else, a pillar for my dad. The one to hold him together. I'll do it for however long he needs, no matter what.

The smile I return to him emits my newfound sense of mission. It's genuine.

It says *I will not fail you.*

"Yes, Dad. We'll do it together."

CHAPTER ONE
Robin

Today

Thursday morning is the time of the week that you just have to have coffee. Heaps of it.

It's that day that isn't the middle of the week and yet feels like miles away from the weekend. You're tired and don't see the light at the end of the tunnel. Helpless to mentally survive this, so you trudge on, and on, and on, and on, and well…

You get my drift.

But it's all right. It's my path to be a strong, independent woman, and I embrace it wholly. I walk in a straight line, gliding past numerous identical cubicles of *B&R Comp* where I intern. I landed as a coder through my hard work at school and the badass interview I passed with flying colors.

All of it was me. No strings pulled by my family, no favors asked.

And even though they knew my last name, I told them I don't want the job if I didn't earn it.

Me and no one else.

As much as I hero-worship my dad and have more money than I know what to do with, I needed this. Had to have the affirmation that I made it in this life in my own right. To add prestige to the Fontaine name instead of clinging to it.

"You're up early."

My fingers flex on my spoon, my palm freezing on the company mug. I suck in a breath, summoning courage.

"Fuck, Dustin, I told you to stop sneaking up on me." I spin toward him, folding my arms over my chest and my not-revealing T-shirt.

My high-neck, black T-shirt covers my cleavage, so the office perv has nothing to see. Doesn't mean that he doesn't try. His brown eyes skate the length of my body, from my face down to my faded jeans and boots.

Always skirting around the edge of sexual harassment, never quite diving in.

"I didn't." He's finally done checking whether my breasts are still the D cup he probably assessed them to be, and the curves of my ass haven't changed since yesterday. "I'm in the break room; you're in the break room. I mentioned how nine a.m. is unusually early for you. No sneaking up on you involved."

Turning my back on the thirty-something-year-old who worked here for years would be rude. Driving my fist to his nose wouldn't be too great for my future in the company, either. I tap my boot on the granite floor, restraining myself through the soothing sound.

"My professor called in sick, class got canceled." Maybe my explanation will appease him, and he'll turn his shaggy, blond, a-la hipster head on me and get back to work.

It doesn't.

Dustin takes a step closer, his I'm-flirting-with-you-if-you-haven't-noticed grin fully intact. As long as we're into body language, I puff out my chest, giving him my best that's-enough glare.

He stays put. Unfortunately, so does his grin.

"Thought you were making up for tomorrow."

I ransack my brain for why I wouldn't be able to work the afternoon tomorrow, coming up blank. "Tomorrow?"

"Yes." He tilts his head, eyeing me like you would a silly girl. Fuck him. "The company's anniversary celebrations?"

"Oh, right, that."

The fakest smile you could possibly imagine tugs at my lips. I have no intention of going, which is probably why I forgot it in the first place. With a month to the end of the semester, I work harder to start memorizing the material for my classes. Anything less would result in me being overwhelmed later.

The company's party lies at the bottom of my priority list.

Though I can't flat out admit that. The family event excuse always works better in most cases, even if we haven't had one in a while.

I shake off Dad's gloomy face and Mom not bothering to answer her phone, stick to my smile, and lie. "It's just that I have this thing—"

"The *mandatory* celebrations," he deadpans.

Fuck. Fuck, fuck, fuck, fuck.

Another uncomfortable notion sweeps through me. This guy allows himself to push the inappropriate boundaries when he's sober. What would he be like when he's drunk? I internally cringe, repulsed, and caged and not fucking happy in the slightest.

What can I possibly say to stop this? Stop him?
Think fast, Robin.

"Then I'll tell my boyfriend we're moving our one-year anniversary celebrations to the company party."

Mental high-five!

Dustin frowns at my blindside strike. "He can't come. It's a no-spouse event."

My mind preoccupies itself with the task of *Where the hell am I going to find a date?* ignoring the sore loser altogether.

"I'm sure they'll make an exception. It's our anniversary too. I can't be expected to leave him at home." I saunter past Dustin, holding the coffee in one hand and pushing the glass door with the other.

Before I leave, I turn my head, winking at him to accentuate my smugness and maybe kick him a little further from me. "If it'll bother anyone, we could just, you know, sneak into a dark corner. Have a good one!"

I rush off to my cubicle, thrusting my coffee to the side of my desk. The pick-me-up drink and my long list of assignments are being put on hold until I find a *date*.

First person I text is my sister Adele.

Me: *Do you know anyone who'd want to date me?*

Adele: *Sorry, the Fontaines don't do desperate. You must have the wrong number.*

Among many similarities between us, our blond hair and sense of humor are the most prominent.

Me: *Very funny, little witch. I have a work socializing event tomorrow and all my team are bringing their significant ones. I don't want to be left out.*

I hide the fact it's a no-spouse event, or that Dustin has been creeping me the fuck out. He hasn't actually done anything besides being an asshole. Mentioning it will do nothing but upset her. The last two months have been plenty strenuous on both her and dad, and it'll be selfish to throw my issues into the mix.

For the second time in the past two months.

Adele: *I thought those were supposed to be no-spouse-ish? Dad's always were.*

See, I wasn't wrong about calling her a little witch. An observant one at that.

Me: *Ours is.*

Adele: *Oh, okay. Anyhoo, don't think about it like you'll be left out. You're an independent badass, it'll only solidify that.*

Me: *And if I want to blend in for once?*

Adele: *You do you. I still can't help though. You know how I feel about men in general after what She-Devil did. I prefer my heart in one piece, thank you very much.*

Me: *You and me both. Also, I miss you. Are you visiting anytime soon?*

Adele: *Miss you guys back. Do you think Dad will be in a visiting mood this weekend?*

Me: *He's getting there. I'll stop by later, see how he's doing.*

Adele: *Thanks. I'm sorry most of it is on you.*

My nose scrunches, overflooded by emotion. Dad isn't a *task*, a responsibility dragging me down. He's our father, and I love him to death. But I get Adele's point, and I appreciate her for it.

Me: *Stop it. Besides, he's getting better every day. It's really more bonding than taking care of him.*

Adele: *I'll sleep over at his place on Spring Break.*

Remi, my boss, coughs on her walk past my table.

"Morning." I grimace, my face apologetic. "Family emergency."

Her reproach wanes. A month ago, after my added fuckedness to my fucked-up life, I broke down in her office and cried. Totally unprofessional. Completely uncontrollable, too.

"Is everything okay with your father?" She pats down the sides of her burgundy blouse for invisible dust.

Remi is the definition of clean and organized, characteristics that make working for her that much easier. The order of our tasks also helped me get through the last couple of months, and for that I'm ever grateful for her.

"Yes, thank you. The usual, you know."

"I'm sorry. I hope the party tomorrow will change that, at least for a couple of hours."

The goddamn party.

I groan on the inside, smiling on the outside. "Looking forward to it."

"Good." Her curt nod signals the conversation is over. "I'll be in my office, then."

"And I'll be here." I widen my smile, repeating our usual retort, then watching her go away.

Me: *You really don't have to. He's much, much better.*

"Psst."

My attention diverts to Winnie, one of my teammates, who peeks her head behind her adjacent cubicle. Her worried black eyes are partly covered by her mass of black hair with purple highlights, searching my face.

"Wanna talk about it?"

Nervous of a wandering Dustin, I sneak glances to left and right and behind my shoulder to cover all my bases. "I need a date for one night. For tomorrow."

She tilts her head, looking for an explanation which I supply in more whispers.

"Ugh, that creep," she says louder than I would've liked.

"Shh."

"Yeah, wouldn't want his precious feelings getting hurt, wouldn't we?" Her disgusted tone emphasizes her equally disgusted eye roll. "Anyway, no can do, sorry love. Scott's last single friend proposed about a month ago."

"Fuck."

"Don't worry, you got us." She ruffles my hair and I swat her hand away. "I'll tell Scott his boys' night is canceled and he's on bodyguard duty."

"It's a no-spouse event," I grit out.

"So how are you bringing a quote-unquote boyfriend?"

"I told Douchebag Dustin it's our anniversary."

Winnie flips her hair back. "It can be ours too."

"No, just no." The idea of a scene that'll paint both me and her in a bad light sucks just as much as punching a drunk Dustin. "I'll manage."

I won't.

"Then again…" The grin her lips curve into has mischief infused into it. In spades.

I ignore it, past the point of caring about the devilish nature of her suggestion. My date could come in a penguin suit for all I care, as long as his penguin hand-wings would be a shield between me and Dustin.

"Go on."

Her black-purple hair disappears, replaced by sounds of drawers opening and shutting.

My curiosity grows and evolves by the second, until she jumps up again. There's a gold business card in her raised hand, and in a blink, she throws it on my desk.

I pick it up, reading the black script lettering. *Into the Night.*

"It's an exclusive bar for the wealthy. A private one." She supplies the answer to the question I must have written on my face. "Scott's Dad left it in their kitchen by accident. I… borrowed it for whenever Mr. Fontaine would be up to go out and maybe start dating again."

"Aww, Win." Emotion rises high behind my eyes, restrained solely by my unwillingness to cry at the office a second time around.

"*Aww* nothing. That's what friends are for." Two girls from QA walk toward the kitchen through our cubicles, their sight forcing Winnie and me into temporary silence.

"Try them out tonight. I'm sure there'll be a silver fox willing to be your fake date and maybe a little bit more…" She wags her eyebrows.

It isn't such a horrible idea, come to think of it. There has to be at least one single, decent-looking man there. The world won't end if I offer him dinner in exchange for being rescued, then go back home and study. By Saturday, this'll all be behind me.

"A date," I say absentmindedly.

"Boring."

"Has anyone told you how sweet you are?" Leaning forward, I pinch Winnie's cheek like an old aunt. "I'll text you after I'm done."

"Done as in *done?*"

"Done as in at home after a date." I groan in humor, dropping back to my chair. "Let me work, woman."

She groans, a real one, and I laugh.

It's only a date. Only a date.

CHAPTER TWO
Robin

I could've gone to HR to report Dustin. It would've been far less stressful than standing here on the curb, looking from the outside into the black window of the *Into the Night* club.

Far less helpful for my reputation in the firm as a crybaby, too.

But really, what am I doing *here*? True, *Into the Night* is mysterious, thus protecting the privacy of its clients. Then again, doesn't *into the night* usually hint at sex?

It does.

Fuck Dustin for not backing off and forcing me to go through this.

I resist the urge to bite my nails while standing in front of the heavy-looking iron door. My little black dress suddenly feels too short, the heels I wear to every social event feeling too high. Nothing is comfortable.

I should go.

No, I'm not chickening out of it. I'm here, I have a mission, and I'll be damned if I return home without a date.

Raising my fisted palm, I knock like I was instructed over the phone. I called ahead to make sure they'll let me in, provided them with my real name too. It only made sense to deduce the fact that they'll ask for my ID later, so I told them the truth.

After hearing the *Fontaine* name, they said they don't need further details, promising me absolute secrecy. And thank fuck for that.

It's bad enough Winnie stole from Scott's dad, but to have them call him?

Gah.

One, pause. Two, pause. One, pause.

The door cracks open. It's dark inside, and the music is almost muted behind a red-haired woman who greets me. She wears a black pantsuit, holding a tablet with an expression that's half friendly, half strict. Professional.

"Good evening. Your name, please?"

"Robin Fontaine."

Her polite smile widens, and she ticks something on her tablet. "Wonderful."

She steps back inside, ushering me inside.

I hesitate, glancing to the sides. What am I doing here?

"You can come in now, Miss Fontaine."

"Okay, thanks."

If it's good enough for Scott's dad, it should be good enough for me. Hopefully.

My heels click on the hardwood floor as I follow the hostess. It takes my eyes a few seconds to adjust to the dim lights of the hallway, and my pace is slow compared to her long, elegant strides.

"We're here." She pauses next to another iron door, clicking on a set of numbers.

The alarm buzzes, and the door opens on its own. Inside the club, the music blares in loud, sensual beats, and the green lights help me see the hostess somewhat better.

"Welcome to *Into the Night.*" She raises her voice to be heard over the music. "I hope you enjoy your night."

Before I walk inside, I have a question I need answered. I step closer to her. "Umm…"

"Yes, Miss Fontaine?"

My teeth nearly bite my bottom lip. I remember my lipstick and stop. "This is my first time here."

"We're well aware."

Eva Marks

"Am I..." I move closer to her, hiding from the view of the man I see twirling a glass of whiskey in his hand in the back. "Is it *that* kind of club?"

There's a sparkle behind her green eyes. "Not unless you want it to be."

"What does that mean exactly?"

"Technically, *Into the Night* is a club just like any other. You have a dancing area, sitting area, and the bar itself." The twinkle in her eye appears as she adds, "There are also private soundproof booths for getting to know someone better. Romantically, or otherwise."

Doubts flutter in my stomach. Then again, I know they know who my dad is, the damage I can cause should anyone here harm me.

"Anything else?"

"No." I stifle my agitation, erecting myself to my full height.

"Enjoy your evening, then, Miss Fontaine."

"Thank you." I pave my way inside, my interest peaking as I scan the patrons sitting or standing or dancing.

I'm not sure what I expected, but they look... normal. There are men and women, younger and older alike. Most of them wear suits or tight dresses, all of them appearing to be successful and confident.

I scan the area for the private booths the hostess talked about. There's a line of more iron doors across the longest wall of the bar. Maybe it's the music, maybe it's the anonymity and independence I experience from being here on my own. But I'm a bit thrilled at the concept.

Even though I won't do anything sexual inside it.

It's hard enough to even think about flirting with someone, when I'm in love with another man.

Callum.

It's been over two years since he moved to Los Angeles. A mere few short weeks after I realized my feelings for him had evolved from innocent sentiments to much darker ones.

I've never loved a man before, not even Xander whom I had sex with in the tenth grade. I do, however, love Callum.

So, as curious as I am to check out exactly what goes on behind the mysteriously closed doors, I pass on that idea.

The dance floor is a no go, too. My motoric skills are practically nonexistent. I'll end up tripping all over myself, which I doubt will get me a date.

Occupying a low table alone just seems wrong and sad. I abdicate that option as well.

Which leaves me with the bar. I run my hands through my hair, mimicking the hostess's self-assured stride as I head over there. The stool in the far-left corner appeals to me the most. I'm more confident than I had been walking in here, but not that confident that I can sit in the center.

"Evening." A blond bartender around my age offers me a polite smile and the drinks menu. "If you'd like anything that isn't on the menu, let me know. My name is Sofia."

"Robin." I smile back, lowering my eyes to the notebook she's passed me.

The black wrapping is silky to the touch, and the white papers inside are thick and rich looking. The name of any sort of alcoholic beverage is written in classic script lettering, none of which interest me.

"Sofia?" I call out to her, intending to ask if they have any virgin drinks.

She stands at the other end of the bar, wiping off glasses. My first instinct is to hop off the stool and walk over to her.

I have one foot down to the floor. My eyes are still fixed on the bartender, but my body is being pulled elsewhere. The hairs at the back of my neck stand on end, and my tummy twists in a strange sensation.

I'm being watched.

Walking to anywhere other than the private booths will lead me closer to the person eyeing me. It'll make my life easier if someone strikes up a conversation with me and I don't have to actively seek it.

Why the fuck not?

Better get it over with, YOLO and all that shit.

I put my other foot down, adjusting the skirt of my dress so I can walk forward without flashing the entire room.

But I don't get past the first step. My face clashes into a wall of a body and my shoulders are being gripped by two equally firm hands.

A scream lodges in my throat, my palms ball into fists, ready to fend off the man who obviously feels too comfortable to touch me.

"Robin?"

Then I look up.

It's not just any man.

It's Uncle Callum.

Fuck.

CHAPTER THREE
Callum

"I thought I recognized you."

The words are a lie. A blatant fucking lie. Seeing the top of Robin's head is more than enough for me to point her out in a crowded room.

The beautiful, smart woman with the most sensual curves in New York. Hell, in the entire world if I had to bet.

She's the woman I'm dying to touch.

The woman I'm not allowed to look at.

Not the way I have the past two years.

My best friend's daughter.

"Uncle Callum." The name grates on my nerves and turns me on in equal measures.

It's an endearment name, sure. It's also the one I imagined her calling me during the long months I fantasized about her riding my cock. For two years when I abstained from being with any other woman. I couldn't, not when my heart was so invested in Robin.

I can't have her. Which is why I moved from Manhattan to Los Angeles just before her eighteenth birthday. Edwin, the other managing partner of our law firm, agreed to switch easily.

Most people raised an eyebrow when I announced it, but the excuse of needing more sunshine and wanting to try surfing seemed to appease them. It was easy, almost too easy. The perfect cover to keep my filthy thoughts away from Robin Fontaine and weekly weekend dinners or lunches with her and her family.

Despite the bad rep criminal lawyers get, I actually have a strict set of morals I've followed throughout the majority of my adult life. Like not representing people I'm confident are guilty of the violent crime they're accused of.

Or wanting to love and ravage the girl, now a woman, who calls me Uncle Callum.

I would've stayed in Los Angeles for a lifetime, too. If I didn't have more urgent business here, in the form of my best friend breaking down.

Wes. Who also happens to be Robin's father.

We've known each other since childhood, celebrated more holidays and gone on more family vacations than I had with my own parents. After my mother and father's tragic passing in a skiing accident when I was barely twenty, Wes practically adopted me.

I'm indebted to him, and that's why I'm here again. We're a unit, him and me. When one of us goes under, the other will always—fucking always—be there.

That includes, unfortunately, his wife leaving him. The day I received Robin's panicked call and the following text of how her mom skipped to Monaco with her high school crush—gag—I was on the first flight out here. Thank fuck for Edwin being able to arrange the change so swiftly and willing to stay in Los Angeles until this mess is resolved.

Until I meet with Wes, see he's alive and functioning. The fact that he hasn't taken my calls did little to hinder my resolve, which ended up bearing fruit. After last week's message where he thanked me for sticking around and said he might be up to get together soon, I'm feeling optimistic.

I'm not stepping a foot into JFK a second before that.

Honestly, I don't want to step a foot outside of this club, now that she's here.

Even the half step back I take so she won't press into my growing length costs me.

"What are you doing here?" she asks.

While the majority of the club's patrons are here for private, sexual encounters or meeting someone who's been vetted by the owners and isn't a creep, truth is, I haven't. "Grabbing a drink. I needed to unwind after work."

"No." Her lips scrunch in that adorable, pensive way of hers. "Here, as in Manhattan. Dad didn't tell me you're visiting."

Gazing down at Robin, catching her citrusy scent and a hint of her cleavage, I'm not interested in discussing her father. Protecting her from strangers who'll want to put their hands on the woman that should be with me—that shit occupies my mind.

"Where's your friend?" I counter, free of judgment. Just… worried. And fucking greedy for her.

There's something about our enclosed, dark surroundings that detaches us from the outside world. From what's right and what's wrong. From the moral barriers that have kept my need for her at bay.

"I'm…" she starts, stepping closer to me.

Her chest brushes the lapels of my dark-blue suit jacket, and her eyes twinkle.

When her tongue darts out to swipe across her bottom lip, I can tell I'm not the only one with decadent thoughts.

Eva Marks

Since she neared her eighteenth birthday, I sensed that change about her. Sensed how she sought me out more often, sat a bit closer on every Christmas and spring vacation we went on together as a family.

It's the reason I haven't told her or her sister I'm here. As much as I'm worried about them and Wes, meeting Robin in person was dangerous.

It is dangerous.

And too late.

In the intimacy the club provides us, the reclusiveness from the outside world and its repercussions, I lift my hand to caress her cheek. It's smooth as I dreamt it to be, and I sink my fingers deeper into her hair. She reacts to me as if we've been doing it for years, leaning into my palm, fluttering her long lashes at me.

I lower my head, an inch or two separating our lips. "You're what?"

Her breath hitches. "I… I'm here alone."

"Is that so?" I wonder for the whole of a half a second why a woman who could have any man she chooses at her feet is here by herself.

"Yeah." Eyes as wide as saucers stare back at me. "Alone."

Then I realize I don't give a fuck. She's a free woman.

But *I* found her. No one else. For tonight, for as long as I can have her, Robin is *my* woman.

"Robin." One of my arms envelops her back. The lack of inhibitions this place provides drives me to slink my palm to her ass and pin her to my hardening cock.

"Don't call me that." She shakes her head, her forehead brushing against mine. "We can't do it. You're right, I'm Robin and you're Uncle Callum… We can't. Dad."

Robin spins in my arms, about to bolt. I'm faster, though. Both my arms snake around her body, my lips trace the length of her neck.

"Shh," I tell her in the authoritative tone I've been using for years. "I can call you something else. We can be other people here. If that's what you want."

"Just for tonight?" Her body relaxes by some.

"Just for tonight, baby." The bite I give her earlobe entices a gasp from her. "You'll be Robin, and I'll be C. Tomorrow we can go back to being our old selves."

I probably won't ever be able to be my old self again once I've touched her. I don't see a way to live with myself without doing it, either.

"Okay." Her head twists, lips nearly touching mine. "Let's be other people. Only for tonight."

CHAPTER FOUR
Callum

One of the attendants approaches us once I signal him, I'd like to have a key. I haven't done it in the past, haven't had the need to, but as a lawyer I have a good eye for detail. I'm observant. Tonight alone I've seen more than five couples do the exact same sign, then be escorted to one of the back doors.

The man who approaches us is in his mid-twenties. He doesn't say a word besides, "Follow me, please," and "Enjoy your stay," as he unlocks one of the doors in the middle of the row, ushering us in.

No one has given us the slightest odd stare, regardless of how much older I look next to Robin. It might be the place. It might be that loving her isn't that fucking terrible.

Then again, none of those people are her dad.

Robin tenses a bit, her softness turning rigid.

I turn off my conscience momentarily. These thoughts are counterproductive. If I surrender to them, Robin will too. The night will be ruined before it starts.

And fuck, do I want it. So many months of buildup, and I finally have her. Willing. Wanting me back.

For this not to crash and burn to the ground, I have to assume control of the situation.

Of her.

"I don't want you to talk unless spoken to." I slither my hands up her soft stomach, up her breasts. She gasps, and I catch that sharp intake of air by pressing both my palms to her throat. "I just want you to listen."

The more I touch her, the more I command her, the more turned on I am. I always envisioned what it would be like to dominate her in this compromised position, other than our daily interactions.

Robin has always been extremely obedient around me. She started flirting with me after her eighteenth birthday—flipping her hair, flashing less-than-innocent smirks to me when no one was watching.

The combination was downright dangerous. I ignored it the best I could, separated us to the best of my capabilities.

Thank fuck I don't need to do that anymore.

"Okay."

My eyes are fixed on her slightly parted lips, the pink hue of them, and my fingers gravitate there. The warm light of the candles spread all across the room illuminates her face in a warm glow, unlike the green party strobes outside in the club.

She's stunning, her beauty accentuated when my middle finger dips into her mouth.

Her tender moan reverberates to my chest. I slide my finger across her lips, reveling in how her slick tongue slips out to taste me.

"Close your eyes, ignore the candles, the scents, even my cock pressed to your thigh." My other hand cups her breast possessively, acting on my fantasies while providing Robin the assurance that I know what I'm doing. "Shut them all out and just focus on what I'm telling you to do."

She listens, closing her eyes, surrendering to me. It's beyond surreal to have my dreams come to life. But it's happening. And I don't waver, not for a second.

I'm getting off on being the authoritative figure, the guide, the one who'll take her to places she couldn't dream of. I crave to own Robin's trust and repay it in arousal. In a breakout of goosebumps. In mind-blowing orgasms.

In care and affection.

By doing everything my sick mind has concocted for her and me for years.

"That's a good girl."

I twist her to the side, and swoop her up in the air. Her eyes remain closed on the walk to the king-sized bed in the center of the room, her breaths shallow.

The hard-on this girl gives me… Fuck.

Lowering her to the bed, I place Robin on her back and spread her knees to the side. Her black panties are exposed, the one thin layer hiding her pussy from me.

From inside my breast pocket, I pull out a lighter, flicking it open.

"You asked us to be strangers, correct?"

Her eyelids move.

"Na-ah." I snap the zippo shut, opening it again. "I said eyes shut."

"Yes." She scrunches them immediately. "Yes to both."

"Very good." The zippo flips open, coaxing a moan out of Robin.

A smile grazes my lips. I knew it. I fucking knew it. This girl, who's so compatible with me, also shares my kink. She responds to the ASMR, arching her back for it, grabbing the sheets.

I snap shut the zippo a second time. I snap it open again, then spin the roll of the wheel. *Tsss*, the gas lights into a flame.

Close, open, roll, *tsss*.

The fourth and fifth times go by in a flash. I'm quick to repeat the movements I've practiced for years, even though I don't smoke.

Robin's silence and complete surrender, despite how unorthodox what I'm doing is, is akin to her rubbing her slick, dripping pussy on my bare cock.

A tease that's the closest thing to fucking, that takes you to the very edge of the cliff.

"So." My hand fists my cock on top of my pants. "The rules for tonight, for us to be strangers, is that I won't touch you any more than I already have. I will, however, do everything in between. You'll come today. You and me both."

The dance of my hand and the zippo isn't disrupted by me talking and jacking off. Flicked open, shut. I hold my thumb on the zippo's wheel, not giving Robin what she so clearly aches for.

Her mouth produces equally sensual sounds, and each of her dragged-out breaths rings so loud there might as well be drums rolling inside my room.

It's deafening, and as I said—I'm a greedy fuck when it comes to her.

I count down to ten in my head, then spin the wheel.

She lifts her ass off the bed, head thrashing to the side. A primal movement, one that emanates from a woman who didn't expect a flick of a lighter to turn her on like that.

"Ah, we're getting somewhere."

"I'm sorry." Her voice becomes muffled when she hides her face behind her palms.

She isn't shy with anyone else. She's just more reserved around me, always has been. Unbelievably adorable, indescribably seductive.

My eyes eat up her shiny blond hair, her slender fingers and black nail polish.

My Robin. For the night.

"Don't be sorry." The zippo goes back into my breast pocket, relieving my hand to play with her some more. "It gets me so fucking hard when you moan. You have my permission to do it all you like, Robin."

I lower myself to the bed beside her. The mattress dips at my weight, and I can tell she's straining to hold still. I bring both of my hands near her ear, tapping my silver rings against each other.

Pinky to pinky, ring finger to ring finger.

Middle, index, thumb.

Thumb, index, middle, ring, pinky.

Her neck arches, baring to me her delicate throat. I look for other artifacts to heighten her sensations, snatching a plant from the nesting table next to the bed and placing it on the mattress.

When my fingernails scratch on it, I let both of us imagine my fingers clawing at her skin. How her flesh would sink beneath the pressure I'll apply to dent it.

A loud *snap* of Robin's palm hits the bed like a whip. A choked whimper slips through her lips next. I don't wait to tap my ring finger in a constant rhythm on the pot.

Like I would tap on what must be her pretty little clit.

Unable to hold back, I stroke myself once in my ache for her, sliding it soundlessly on the fabric.

I'm not moaning or grunting either.

Completely fucking quiet.

The sound of the touch that'll let her know I'm stroking myself will have to wait.

This one is only for myself, to take the edge off so I can focus on her.

"You doing okay?" My finger taps on the mattress beside her ear.

She grunts, her nipples poking from under her dress. "Y-yes."

"You want to touch yourself?"

"No." She sobers up fast. "Not me."

"So, you're wet down there, have to be"—I bring on a short string of taps on the pot that make her back arch and her breath hitch in her throat—"turned on, clit swollen, and you're refusing to touch yourself?"

"I—yes."

"That's not an acceptable answer." Not wasting a moment to hear another reply I won't like, I demand, "Do it."

"It's embarrassing."

"Quiet."

Robin falls silent. I unbuckle my belt, knowing what the sound will do to her. I won't lay a finger on her, but she sure as shit will.

"You listening to what I'm doing?"

She gulps, a clear sound in the void surrounding us.

"I'll take that as a yes."

My cock is hard, balls heavy. I don't seek release, though. Won't do it unless she asks me to. Begs for it.

But I do take action, lowering my cheek to hers and grunting low and gravelly in her ear. She moans in return, her breaths coming out in quick, short puffs.

"You like what you hear?" My lips brush the shell of her ear just barely.

"Yes."

"Are you going to be good and touch yourself?"

A short pause, followed by a, "I can't. Please."

"Want me to make you come?"

"Fuck. Yes. I do." She sighs, slipping down on the bed, raising her skirt up to her waist, thinking I'll give in to her like I usually have. "I'm ready."

Saliva pools at my mouth from seeing the dark spot in the center of her panties.

And still, I don't move.

"I won't go near your wet little pussy, Robin unless you do as I say. Touch. Your. Self."

"Okay," she mumbles, seeing there's no other option.

With a shaky movement, her hand drifts lower, briefly passing the mounds of her breasts, diving beneath her underwear.

"Rub it." I tap the ring on my finger on the plant to emphasize my request. "Rub your clit for me."

My cock jerks from having her so close to me, from watching her do what I demanded and pleasuring herself.

"What a good girl you are," I praise her for her efforts. For being so fucking perfect. Just as she's always been.

And I don't stop there. The sound of my belt being pulled out of the loops, slipping along the fabric of my pants, is enough to make her moan again. It's a choked moan, revealing her struggle to give in to me completely.

Her timidness and need clash, and I'm here to catch the relics of it.

As soon as she breaks down completely.

A process I'm all too keen to speed up, for both her and myself. I'm going to milk every ounce of our encounter, while I give it back to her tenfold.

"Moan for me." I'm not subtle, my commands becoming more harsh as my desire grows. "Again. Louder this time."

The whimper I hear does not satisfy the animal Robin woke in me.

"I'll make"—*crack*, ring meeting pot—"a symphony of"—one, two, three snaps of my fingers—"noises to make you come. But you have to be my siren in return."

She moans, then. Slow and steady. And still being maddeningly quiet about it.

This. Is. Not. Enough.

I take the potted plant.

And I bash it against the nearest wall.

CHAPTER FIVE
Robin

This wasn't the plan. To lie here with one hand massaging my clit to the precipice of coming, to have my nipples so hard they poke through my bra.

With Callum, out of every other man in New York.

The man that not only do I love, but that does things that I don't think I'm halfway equipped to handle. What this man is doing to me should be deemed illegal. Yes, illegal, right up there with murder in the first degree.

How else can I explain to myself, or anyone, the throaty, pleasured cry he coaxes out of my lips? Or how my hips buckled from the sound of the plant crashing into the wall?!

The need he stirs in me is so primitive I hardly recognize myself. But I can't help it.

This isn't just the hot-as-fuck ASMR kink. Not just how the sounds he makes play on all my pleasure centers as if I were his violin.

It's more, so much more.

It's everything about him.

The confidence. The use of sounds to reach me.

The voice I remember and came for many times in the past.

Uncle Callum's voice.

He's my dream man, the one I can never have yet I'm desperate for.

He promised me one night. He promised we'll keep it as detached as possible.

But it's bullshit. Because even as he calls my name, even though my eyes are encapsulated by darkness, I'm hyperaware of the man beside me.

The man I'd spent days with at the open kitchen in the Hamptons, with one particular memory that keeps replaying in my head from over a year ago.

"Hey, Robin." Callum stepped out of the guest bedroom, wearing blue jeans and a white T-shirt that clung to his broad chest.

"Hi." I waved at him from where I leaned behind the kitchen island. I could've waited in my room until Adele and my parents were ready.

Then I wouldn't have been alone with him. Which I should've aimed for, to tame this need. Problem was, it was unstoppable.

He looked around the kitchen and spun his head to the living room, running a hand through his damp hair. "No one's ready? Didn't we say eight?"

"Nope and yes." My noncommittal shrug was an act. On the inside, a thousand bees buzzed at the prospect of being alone with Callum. Even for a few minutes.

He shrugged back, his mouth twisting. "I'm going to wait on the deck, listen to the ocean. Care to join me?"

Did I want to breathe? Very much. The air he's breathing? Even more so.

"Yes, please."

"After you." He slid the door open, and we were out.

Standing there, even three feet apart from him, had my belly in knots. Our gazes were trained at the sand and the waves, the both of us quiet in an unnerving way. Like I felt before I had my first kiss.

Knowing Callum would never be my second kiss, I forced myself to break the awkward silence.

"So, umm. How was your day?"

"I'm not that interesting." He maintained his gaze ahead of him. Before I had a chance to object and tell he was the most interesting man I'd ever

met, he said, "The ocean is far more interesting, though. Close your eyes, Robin. Listen to it."

And I adhered to this simple command. I stood, listened, and crammed down my desire.

A seriously difficult task when he added in his deep, teaching-like voice, "Doesn't it make you feel?"

Yeah, it made me feel alright. And then I felt a whole lot more in my room at night.

Having the past and present mingle into one, I don't just feel it, I *live* it.

He allows me the space to experience it, free of consequences. This isn't really us, and this is where it'll end. All I have left to do is sit, or lie back in my case and enjoy the ride.

Enjoy moaning for a man who longs to hear it. Who urges me to touch myself. I finger myself, wetness coating my finger, and I let out a soft cry.

"That's more like it." The gratification in his voice is smooth, same as the sound of him removing his belt.

Everything about this man is calculated. From his demands down to the destruction of the plant or something heavy enough to rock the walls the way it had.

His palm makes a thumping sound on the bed again. The idea of him tending to my pleasure, of thinking about it before his, drives me even crazier with desire.

It also informs me he's close to me. So close. My eyes roll with every wave of my desire, my hair hanging behind the cushion as my head drops back on the bed.

"What does your finger do inside your cunt?"

He gives me so much, I'm more than willing to return the favor now.

I answer through my mortification, for him. "Touching myself."

"Come on, Robin. You know me." He's not reproaching me. He draws the words out slowly, seducing me with each syllable. "I'm not a fucking teenager. Tell me explicitly, where is your hand?"

"My pussy."

"Fingering your hot little cunt?"

His fingers scratch a fabric, which I'm assuming is his shirt. The sound of the stroke is long, and my head runs with me as I picture his broad, flat man's chest.

Suddenly, I don't just want to return a favor. I want to please him completely. To be desirable. I want to make him want me like mad, too.

Like I'll never be able to do in the outside world.

"Yes."

"Mmm." His hum sends a fresh new spike of arousal to my core.

I half moan, half cry out. Stroking and stroking and stroking.

"You're wet, aren't you?"

He wraps his words in silk, infusing them with the power to verbally fuck me. And they do. God, how they do.

"Yes."

"Tear your panties off." His hand slams on the mattress again. "Let me see the fabric tear. To have your pussy exposed to me."

Callum turns me into a beast with how much I need him. I don't mind that he's watching anymore. I live to be wanted by him, gripping the waistband of my panties and tearing them off my body.

"Look at you, such a good girl, doing as you're told." A hollow thumping fills the pause of his speech.

Is it his cheek? Where his light stubble shows? If I just forget about my dad and the guilt for a second and be Robin, would he touch me? Go down on me? Will the hair on his face leave burn marks on my thighs?

I can't forget, though, and my conscience will tear me to pieces if I'll allow something like that to happen. It's bad enough that I'm losing myself in C. It'll be far worse to strip off the veil of make-believe and turn this into a very real reality.

"Make a sound for me, baby," he growls. "A sound I can't make. A sound I *need* to hear."

"Anything," I answer the man who is and isn't there.

I'm not the compliant type. With anyone other than him. He guides me through hidden nooks of my soul's forest I wouldn't have stepped foot in otherwise.

"Spread your legs. Shove three fingers into your sopping hole. Up to the last knuckle." The dirty command is embellished by his sexy intonation. "Let me hear that suction when they disappear inside you."

As much as I want to please him, as warm and needy as his demand turns me into, I'm scared. I'm nervous about exposing this sound, such a private part of my sexuality.

I hesitate a second longer than he's willing to wait.

He repeats the slam on the bed. I feel it all the way down to my bones.

Aroused by it.

"Do it."

He leaves me no other choice.

I don't need any other choice.

I do it, giving C the sound he asked for.

"Yes," he grunts, manly and feral.

This is another one of the rare sounds he's let that sound anything like pleasure. Like he's shifting into a state where he's not fully in control of himself.

The bossy side of him is a major turn-on; it's what drew me to him in the first place, what drives me to plunge my fingers deep repeatedly.

And yet… this glimmer of his untethered-self pushes me to find out what it'd be like to have him spiral.

To have us both spiraling together.

Just as I think that, his fly rolls down.

I stop fucking myself, curling my fingers inside me and teasing my walls, listening to him.

"Are you?…" My voice trails, ending in a shallow breath.

He chuckles, rugged and low. There's no mocking edge to it. It's more of an embrace. Akin to what a slow lick of his tongue down where my fingers are must feel like.

"No. I'm not jacking off. I'm hard for you, had to have my cock out for you. How does it make you feel?"

In the haze of my arousal and the faux-anonymity, I shed another layer of shame. "Like I want you to do it."

"Do what?"

My needy body stumbles in this new territory. I'm no match to his dirty talk. I haven't talked to

Callum this way, not even close. I couldn't so much as tell him that a boy kissed me when I was younger.

Now this?

"You know."

"No." His zipper rolls again, in the opposite direction I imagine.

"No!" I'm so close. He can't leave me.

"Then say it. Give yourself over to this experience. To this one night. To me."

"Touch yourself. Touch yourself with me." I gasp at my words.

But I like them. Love the sound of them on my lips.

The obscenity surprises and exhilarates me. My desire releases itself from a part of me I didn't know existed, and I can't be ashamed about it a second longer.

Our filthy talk, added to the sounds that nearly bring me to a brain orgasm, are exactly everything I needed.

"Much better, little Robin."

The zipper rolls in the other direction. I press a thumb to my clit as I return to finger-fucking myself for him, using three fingers as he commanded.

My hips roll; my moans, cries and gasps stream up my lungs and bump into walls of the room we're in.

"So, what are you asking of me?" His rings clink beside my ear like he dropped them in a rain of silver. "To wrap my fingers around my cock?"

He laces the description with a groan. Unbidden, my body responds to him with a moan of its own.

"I'll take that as a yes."

"Please."

He hums in approval. "While you thrust your fingers in your pussy with one hand, pinch your nipple with the other."

He doesn't simply paint a scenario; he orders me to enact it.

"That." I slide my hand up, giving my nipple a sweet twist through my bra. "I want that."

"Want me to tell you what I'm doing, or will sounds suffice?"

"Tell me."

I don't mind that he hears my weakness for him. I'm in too deep to care about anything except me and C. I'm hard and soft and desperate for his voice and his sounds and just him.

He offers me a relief of my responsibilities, of the promises I made, of the wreck our life has become. He knows me better than anyone else, and despite the torment of sorta-making love to Dad's best friend and how awful it is, I'm happy.

Life's safe and downright fucking perfect as long as I'm with him.

"I'm tugging on my dick, Robin."

To keep hearing the nearly inaudible sound of his hand rubbing the flesh between his legs, I bite down my bottom lip. I'm not letting the growl inside me interrupt *this*.

"I go slow, base to tip, rolling my hand. Then faster." The friction sounds match his words and labored breaths. "I slow down again, my thumb massaging the base of my swollen head. I'm so fucking hot for you."

There isn't an inch of skin on my body that isn't covered by goosebumps. He has such a way to my heart and my core.

It's the kind of mouth I'm craving to have on my pussy. A mouth I'm taking the liberty to picture eating me out as I keep touching myself.

"I move up to the head now."

"Yeah." I answer no particular question, stroking my need for him.

It soothes nothing in me, but I keep doing it. Because he told me to. Because his voice is the one thing, I have to navigate through this epic desire ruling my life in this room.

"I rub the drop of precum over my head, down my cock. And I keep stroking it. I'm jerking off to you. Do you hear my hand fucking my cock, wishing it were you?"

He grunts, I grunt. My whole existence morphs into a feral groan of pleasure.

"That's what you do to me, you get my cock so fucking hard."

A thump reaches my ears, the mattress, a little farther now. Since my existence is so in-tune with him, I know it's his free hand meeting the wall.

"My hard-on begs to fuck you. Begs to come to the sound of your wet pussy, of your back scratching on the sheets when I hammer into you."

My orgasm builds brick by brick, threatening to erupt.

As if on cue, he asks, "You close?"

"I am." My toes curl, fingers pinching my other nipple. "I really am."

"But you won't come." He stops pumping his cock, his heavy breathing slowing. "Not before *you* beg for me."

"Please." I'm biting my bottom lip hard, talking through it. "I need you."

"More."

"I want to come."

"I need more of your voice," he says, then returns to being the instructor. "You can do it. Tell me everything you fantasize about in that room, and I'll let you come with me."

"Sadist."

"Siren."

My compliance to him outweighs my rebellious nature and my shame. "I wish I could hear your balls slapping against my cunt when you fuck me from behind."

"I'd slam myself hard into you." Callum twists my dreams into his command, shaping them into something real. He's hitting the wall again and again and again, creating a sound that rings a lot like what I asked him to do. "Going faster the closer you get, the tighter your walls suck me in."

"Can I come?" I don't know what propels me to ask for permission. My impulses speak for me, telling me not to just come by myself.

"Not yet." The clapping slowly stops. The silence doesn't last, giving way to the repeated *whoosh* of his hand stroking himself. "More. Tell me more of what you want. What you've wanted all along."

"Your cock deep inside me." My insides coil, my orgasm a relentless force striving to get out. "Your hands smacking my ass if I'm not moaning loud enough for you."

He rewards me by giving me almost what I wished for, his palm landing on my thighs, my stomach, creating music with my body.

"I can't anymore," I whine, willing to drop to my knees at his order. "Please come with me."

"Fuck." His hand meeting the mattress now evokes a thunder-like sound.

This time, I know it's not for my pleasure; it's his frustration.

"I'm coming, like you asked me to. Imagine my balls slapping on your cunt, my cock is buried inside you. Come for me, baby, do it."

With his words, I don't just come for him. I scream for him. The desperate cry starts at my pussy as it clenches and comes, bursting up to my stomach, surging to my lungs and out to the room we share.

Callum grunts and curses. To my shame, I picture thick sperm jutting out on Callum's large hand and flat stomach. In my mouth.

The imagery alone elongates my orgasm, and my descent to the earth is stretched out like rubber.

"Hey." His zipper slides; his voice softens.

I'm finally back in my body. Sort of. At least enough to manage a reply. "Hey."

"You did so well."

This kind praise after he forced me miles out of my comfort zone soothes me, warming me from head to toe. Making me feel appreciated and cared for.

I fix my skirt, straightening it down my thighs. Slowly, my composure is regained, which, for some reason, feels important for me. Important that he knows I'm not this little Robin he knew anymore.

"Thank you," I say in my most confident voice, still in the darkness.

He doesn't reply immediately, leaving me to bask in the silence for a bit. "You want to open your eyes?"

My cheeks burn hot. Talking to him now that I'm no longer hungry for sex is suddenly different. Extremely different.

Crap. What do I do?

"It's okay, Robin." The weight on the mattress shifts when he changes position. "Can I ask you something?"

"Sure." My fingers fidget, getting restless by the moment.

"This is not me passing judgment." He sounds like he means it. All his former authority morphs into this confident blanket of kindness he drapes around me. "I'm just curious."

I gulp because, shit. These sentences never end well, no matter how honest he sounds.

"You never told me why you're here." His tone softens, embodying his promise to be understanding.

I could tell him the truth. Ask him to accompany me to the company event. Twelve hours ago, when he was still my Uncle Callum, I probably would've, had I known he's in New York.

We're past that, though. Way, way past that.

He had me losing my mind with his set of sounds, with the voice of a man I've been pining over for years. Him taking me on a fake-date will stoke my need into areas I'm afraid are so deep and dark, I won't ever be able to return.

We already have one heartbreak too many in our family. No need to worsen the situation.

I'll just have to handle Dustin by myself. I'll be fine.

"I heard good things about it, and I was bored at home." My heart clenches in my chest from lying to him.

"You sure that's all there is to it? You can talk to me about everything."

I could. Past tense. "Is it okay if you go outside ahead of me?"

"Yeah." He's a tad resigned, yet not disappointed. He tries his best, I hear it in his voice, to talk to me like he's always used to. "Just remember that whatever it is, I'm always a phone call away. No matter what happened between us tonight, I'm always here for you."

"Thank you."

Then he does as I asked of him. Gets up and walk away.

I should be relieved, but I'm not. My chest tightens as I'm being left to myself, to once more being so fucking lonely.

CHAPTER SIX
Callum

I can't get Robin out of my head. Not the way I talked to her, not the sight of her touching herself.

Yet the worst memory plaguing me isn't sexual. It's her mistrust in me.

We used to be comfortable around each other. Flirtatious over the numbered occasions we had the past two years, that's true. A constant undercurrent of tension kept passing between us for years. Though it's never been uncomfortable or sexual for either her or me.

Mainly because I—the responsible adult who didn't even think of her that way before her eighteenth birthday—have made sure to never go there.

Eva Marks

Our connection hasn't been less than respectful, not once.

When she wanted to talk, I'd been the one to hear her out. When she wanted to pretend to be a sweet girl despite me and the rest of the universe knowing she was a sharp-tongued woman, I let her play that game too.

When she needed grounding, when she'd sit next to me on the deck while the rest were swimming. Our taciturn routine consisted of me ignoring her round breasts bouncing, the water dripping down her bikini on her half-naked body, focusing on the table or the ocean while telling her to sit and listen.

Sit, I'd tell her, and she would perch her curvy ass on the wicker chair beside me.

Listen, I'd instruct her, and she would put her hands in her lap.

In nothing but a bikini, she would both sit and listen to stories from court, about clients I decided not to take because I knew they were guilty. About life in faraway L.A.

We were comfortable together. Safe.

I want it and her back.

Most of all, I want her to not be riddled with guilt by what we've done. It might be what closed her off to me. She shouldn't have to go through this.

I helped her once, two months ago, over the phone. I can help her a second time.

But I need to find her first.

"Garland." I don't even give our law firm's investigator in New York the chance to say hello once he picks up. "Got a second?"

"For you, always." He's outside, judging by the cars honking around him, and other people's chatters reaching to my side of the call. "Talk to me."

"I need you to track someone for me." I have no important meetings or a court hearing tomorrow that calls for heavy-duty preparations. I'm all hers. "To tell me where she's at this very minute."

"Is this a missing person's case? Don't you need the police for these things?" A paper bag shuffles, and he yells to someone on the other end of the line, "Thanks, man."

"Not a missing person."

Normally, I'd explain myself so he'd know what to search for better. That is, if we were talking business.

This is anything but.

"I'm texting you her number. Don't ask any more questions, just fucking find her. Now."

"Can I at least have my breakfast?" he says around a bite.

Eva Marks

I've known Garland for years and his humor. It amuses me most times, when there isn't a cloud of guilt hovering over my head.

"No. Find her."

I terminate the call, texting him Robin's contact without her name. My pen taps restlessly on the modern glass desk in my office.

I still tap it five minutes later, stopped only by the chime of my phone.

"I won't be back for the next two hours," I tell Mabel, my secretary, as I button up my gray suit jacket and head out. "Maybe more. Clear my schedule for today."

She says, "Okay," while I'm already three feet forward to the elevators.

At the parking lot I hop on my H2R motorcycle, put on my helmet, and speed my way downtown.

The short drive from our offices on the Lower East Side to Robin's college passes in a breeze. My motorcycle zooms past taxis, limos, town cars, and other motorcycles—a better guarantee than the Mercedes that I won't miss Robin.

And when I slow down by the gate, I'm pleased to see that I don't.

Even better than not missing her. I catch her right at the gate as she and a friend walk outside. I pull the handle of the bike, parking it at the curb, and step to the pavement and take off my helmet. I rake my fingers through my hair, brush it back while eyeing her before I make a move.

She braided her hair behind her back, walking tall with a messenger bag slung over her shoulder. Her outfit is a classic Robin; dark, high-rise jeans, a distressed gray shirt tucked into them, and her famous dusty leather boots.

You'd never in a million years guess this girl had billions in her name.

You wouldn't guess she ran off half-crying after yesterday's events, either. Her eyes are a reflection of the sunshine, glimmering as she talks to the young woman next to her. There's brightness to her smile. Her laughter is genuine.

What a relief. At the very least, she can put on a show that she's okay.

She's not, not really. I would know. It shows the instant her eyes, as if on a calling, turn to lock onto mine.

Robin frowns, casting her gaze to the concrete. She quiets, fumbling with her bag strap, her cheeks turning a million shades of red.

"Robin?" Her friend nudges her shoulder.

"Yeah?" Robin answers to the floor.

I'm done dancing around this. I take a few steps to face the two of them, offering my hand to the friend. "Nice to meet you, I'm Callum Reinhart. A friend of Robin's dad."

"Hi, I'm Jenna." She shakes my hand, then mouths to me, "What's wrong?"

Robin groans, "I can hear you, Jen. And no, nothing happened."

"Can we talk?" I place a hand on her shoulder. An uncle's gesture.

She doesn't grimace. It's a good sign. So is her, "Fine."

"I'll catch you later." Jenna walks backward, then twists and fades into the throng of people.

I drop my hand the longer she doesn't speak. "Robin."

"What?"

"Look at me."

Today, unlike yesterday, the strong woman who grew up before my eyes doesn't hesitate. Her head tilts up, meeting my inquiring gaze.

"You okay?"

"I'll be fine."

Fuck. That's not okay. "Wanna talk about last night?"

She grimaces without turning from me. She's not okay, no, but she's regained her signature strength.

"Like I promised," I start easy. "Your dad would never know."

This is a promise I won't break, for her and her dad alike. It'll rip his heart right out of his chest in a second. He'll forever have this image ingrained in his brain. He'll never forgive me for it. I should've stopped as soon as I recognized her in the club. I should've been the adult. Should've taken her by her wrist, walked her out, sent her home.

She flinches again.

I'm not helping. Not helping at all.

"You said you needed a favor, Robin." My brow furrows. "I haven't changed. I'm the same Callum I've been for the past twenty years, even if I'm also the person from the club. That's the reality of it. I can't take it back."

Can't take back wanting to be inside you and take you out to dinner, not in that particular order.

"I'm here for you, for anything else. If it's I who upset you, I'd like for you to tell me. If it's anything else, I'm here for it, too."

Her mouth pinches, fingers twisting the bag strap. "Never mind. I can handle it."

I take a step closer, crowding her space and forcing her to look up. "Handle what, exactly?"

It agonizes me that she has no one to turn to. What else has she been carrying on her slim shoulders?

"There's this guy at work I needed help with."

My fury meter shoots through the roof. My palms are tight fists, mind racing to all the ways a body can disappear.

"What. Guy?"

Everyone has the right for legal representation. I, however, don't take on rapists and murderers who I'm positive are guilty. Scum shouldn't walk just because I have a sharp tongue, or the police didn't file the evidence right. It's a conscience thing.

Like it would be to hide the body of the man who touched Robin somewhere in the Bronx River Forest.

Robin leaves the strap of her bag, moving to tug on her braid. "He's no one, really. Just a guy from work."

"You don't ask random strangers for help for a no one." I sigh, controlling my tone. "Why isn't HR doing anything about it?"

I still don't know what *it* is. But if it walks like sexual harassment and talks like sexual harassment, then it's the fucking duck alright. I'm fuming on the inside, hiding the raging pulse behind my eyes to the best of my capabilities.

"I haven't told them."

Any sort of serenity I assumed gets tossed out the window. "What!?"

She winces at my voice. So does a girl who walks by us.

I can't make a scene. Nor can I let this pass quietly. "Why didn't you tell anyone?"

"He's not doing anything," Robin whispers, her face scrunching. "He's in my face all the time, that's all. Yesterday he… um… He gave me the feeling he'd do more than that at the party—didn't say it, but it was there."

"Robin." My anger becomes a vivid thing, like the trees circling her campus.

"I lied. I told him I have a boyfriend and that we planned on celebrating our anniversary, and this is what we'll do instead of the dinner we had to cancel. I was looking for a date, that's it, U—Callum."

The urge to take her in my arms consumes me. I let my words hug her instead. "I'll be your date."

"No, please." Her eyes widen in terror. "I don't need anything from you."

"You won't be asking it from some stranger, or fending for yourself." My teeth grind, jaw tics. "I'm here for you, for your family. Always have been, like you guys were there for me."

Not touching her stops being a valid option.

Although it should. It really fucking should.

Eva Marks

My palm cups her jaw, angling her head higher. Our breaths mingle and, despite it being painfully intoxicating, I focus.

"Wes hasn't been taking my calls—"

Her lust dissolves as shock takes over. "You called?"

"That's why I'm here. Waiting until he's ready." I reason with her in my instructor voice. I don't just say it, I believe it. "Your mom leaving must be the hardest thing that has to have ever happened to him. I can't force my friendship on him. What I can do is be here. And thankfully, he answered."

"He—he never told me you called."

Her gray eyes turn into pools of sadness. My ego wonders whether it's due to the fact that her father had a lifeline of support he neglected to take, or…

No. She couldn't possibly regret our missed opportunity to spend time together. Before yesterday, maybe. Today, she doesn't. As much as I enjoyed her voice, our connection, coming while listening to her orgasm in the other room, I know it's wrong, too.

After all, that's what propelled me to switch offices from here to L.A. a little over two years ago.

She and I were driving out of the city and into the Hamptons for the family's short getaway for Adele's birthday. Her parents filled their car to the brim, and there was only room for one of the two girls to join their ride.

Robin, unfortunately, volunteered to drive with me.

"Uncle Callum." She looked at me from the passenger's side of my Mercedes, her smile as bright as the sun.

Without a care in the world.

I had plenty.

It'd been less than three weeks since I first noticed my newfound feelings for her.

That whenever she flicked her hair back, I wanted to wind it around my hand and pull. That when she took a bite of cake at the dinner her dad had invited me to, I wanted to kiss the chocolate off her mouth.

That when she started talking, I wanted to tell her to keep at it for the rest of my fucking life. I loved her voice. I loved the words she said. I just loved her.

But I couldn't have any feelings for her.

Toward Wes's daughter.

A girl I'd known her whole life.

It shouldn't matter that she grew up to be a young woman. That it'd been less than three months since she'd turned eighteen.

She was Wes's child.

"Yes, Robin?" I quipped.

"Never mind."

And now my actions saddened her. Fucking great.

"I'm sorry, I'm trying to focus on the road. Talk to me."

"Oh, nothing." Her bright attitude returned as if nothing happened. *"I was just wondering if you have any court stories. I haven't heard from you in a while, so..."*

My heart gave a weird thump. She cared. She could've done what most young people her age did, pop her AirPods in her ears and be on her phone for the entire drive.

I cared that she cared.

I talked to her, telling her about my last client and how I helped him get his deserving "not guilty" verdict. She answered, beamed, clapped with enthusiasm.

I fell for her, when all evidence pointed out that I shouldn't have.

It was then that I decided to switch places with Edwin in L.A., vowing never to return.

But I'm here now. We're bound like we were in the club.

We'll just have to deal with it.

"Again, that's his right, Robin. Don't hold it against him."

I take a step back. I allow the both of us air.

"The past is in the past." And I definitely, most fucking definitely, ignore the residue of disappointment on her features. "We have a party to attend tonight."

"It's going to be so awkward." She kicks an invisible rock on the ground.

"We won't let it." I tilt my head, lips twitching in what's supposed to be a smile. "I won't let it."

"Fine. You can come." She huffs out a low breath, straightening up and smoothing down the twisted strap on her shoulder. "Pick me up at eight thirty?"

"You got it."

"Oh, and Callum?" A small devilish grin creeps up her lips, what she's capable of. "You gonna stalk me there too, or are you planning on asking me for my address?"

CHAPTER SEVEN
Robin

This is stupid. This is really fucking off-the-charts kind of stupid.

Not my dress, of course. That one is precious. It holds a sentimental value, a second-hand from Grandma, Dad's mom. She gave it to me a few weeks before the cancer took her.

The sleeves and hem are made of a thin layer of black lace, and the rest of the maxi dress is from black silk. I inherited my grandma's curves, so it sits perfectly on my body. My heart stings a little at her memory, and I wish she was here.

Instead of focusing on how I'm preparing for a party I could've easily avoided.

Although I know it's not true. I don't have the face to be a chicken and hide with such a hero for a father. He's been waking up every morning for the past two months, despite hating his new reality. He's been running his empire, attending video calls, and taking care of business—albeit without leaving his home, but so fucking what, that still counts.

He's done all of it while sadness has been chipping away at his soul.

The evenings I spent at his place, I witnessed first-hand how he'd collapse after he'd ended a workday. Sunk into the sofa, staring into space, talking about nothing, the days he did talk.

Yet he hasn't given up, hasn't let it take him down and came out victorious. These past two weeks, he's been doing better. We shared dinners and watched comedies like *Central Intelligence*, and he laughed. Once, but once counts for a whole fucking lot.

And so, hell to the no. I'm not about to let Dustin run my life and scare me into not attending. School can wait. I can face him.

Thanks to Callum.

The fake date with a not-fake man whom I can never have. Because after Mom left us and what I did to Dad later—even before Callum and I happened—I'd rather die before being the cause of my father's relapse.

The phone rings, jolting me out of my nagging thoughts.

Dad.

I clear my throat, empty the thoughts of Callum out of my voice, and swipe to the right to take the call.

"Dad! Hi." Too cheery. Fuck.

"Robi, are you okay?"

"Yeah, I—uh, I'm getting ready, we have this work party thing."

"Oh, great," he states, lacking enthusiasm.

"I forgot about it myself." A heap of guilt rises due to the lies. And the other thing. "Don't worry, like, at all. I don't plan on drinking."

"Not worried, honey." His love spills into the line, another weight resting heavily on my growing shame. "I'm a little worn out, that's it. You're a good kid. The light of the house. Always have been."

Emotions rise to cloud my vision. I'm not good, I'm a fucking disappointment. First my fuckup a week after Mom bailed on us when I got so drunk, I blacked out and worried Dad to death. Then, even worse, what Un—*fuck! Not Uncle*—Callum and I did.

Yeah, this does not go down in Daddy's good little girl manual. That shit sits in the selfish-asshole realm.

Even more so, since I lie about it by hiding the truth, and deflecting on top of it. "Are you okay, Dad? You've been doing better the last couple of weeks."

"Yeah, Brock was over here this morning, kicking my ass back into shape."

Brock has been Dad's personal trainer for years. Dad didn't consider working out a necessity, as he had with work. He said the company isn't able to go on without him, but his body could. I guess that means my father is finally back.

"Dad, that's amazing! Call me next time, I miss working out together."

"I'll try working around my busy girl's schedule." He laughs, the sound blowing a metaphorical hot-air balloon named *happiness* high up to the clouds. "Anyway, I just wanted to call and tell you good night. Thanks for dropping by yesterday afternoon."

Right before I did the audio version of fucking your best friend.

"Stop it. You know I love hanging out."

"Me too, Robi. I promise I'll be more fun going forward."

"You always are."

The moment I feel like the hot-air balloon delivers me into the softness of the clouds, the sun burns right through me.

Eva Marks

Callum's name flashes on my notification. A short quick message saying, *Hey, waiting under your apartment building.*

"My ride's here."

"Okay, sweetheart. Have a great night."

"Thanks." I hang up, scolding myself for lying as I snatch my purse, put on a black shawl, and slip into my heels.

I keep calling myself a *liar* while running my hands through the hair I let down, then force myself to stop. What happened between me and Callum was a one-time thing. Blowing off years' worth of steam.

In the elevator, I add on another generous portion of logic to slow my self-hatred. Callum isn't here to fuck me or try to hit on me. He's here doing what Uncle Callum does, what the family you choose does; you protect your own.

That's what he said, and the more I repeat it, the more sense it makes.

That's all there is to it.

That is all there is to it.

"Hey." He leans on his black Mercedes.

His stance is casual. My feelings are most certainly not.

Fuck.

I peruse him slowly in an attempt to get a handle on the rapid beats of my heart.

Callum parted his short hair to the side, while still leaving it somewhat voluminous. He wears an indigo blue suit that emphasizes the color of his eyes, and a plain white button-down shirt that stretches across his toned stomach. No tie, no watch, although I know he's got plenty of both. Just the silver rings any biker or rock star could've been donning.

Mesmerizing, breathtaking.

What triggers this flare of affection and emotions in me isn't his objective handsomeness, though. It's his choice of clothes, how he didn't go over the top to flash his wealth.

I suspect, almost sure of the fact, that it's because of me.

He's aware of my dislike for wearing designer clothes for the sake of having a brand's name to show off with. And he matched his style to mine. As my guest, as my chaperone. As my fake boyfriend for the night.

Is there such a thing as too perfect?

If there is, Callum is for sure a strong runner-up for a claim to the title.

"Hi." I wave timidly, the compliant girl I've always been around him.

"You look lovely." He steps back, opening the passenger's door for me.

Eva Marks

"Thank you." My cheeks must be spitting fire like the Targaryen's dragons, with how hot Callum makes me.

Once I'm in, he rounds the car, slides elegantly into the driver's side, and pulls the car into the road. He navigates through Friday night's traffic toward the Financial District where the venue is. Cool and utterly handsome.

He's silent, as if trying to let me decide when I want to speak.

I decide I want to. I also decide I would very much like to keep ignoring the pink elephant in the car named voice-induced-orgasm.

"Thank you again, for going with me."

"Please, Robin." He shifts his attention from the road to my face, hiking up an eyebrow. "Whatever you need, whenever you need it. Call me. First, or second. Or as a last choice, even. Just don't go to strangers. I'm always here for you."

What was supposed to be an innocuous, polite sentence turns out to be the reason for my tummy doing flip flops. "Same."

His lips tug into a smirk. "Fully aware."

Needing to distract myself from him, I browse through the radio stations until I find the opening tunes of "Believer" by Imagine Dragons. The song, which up until this point has been on my top ten all-time favorites, jumps quickly to the respectable first place.

Thanks to Callum, who turns it into a vibration that rolls down my belly and into my core.

He plays his fingers on the wheel to the rhythm of the drums, sending wave after wave of desire to my already wet and needy sex.

His smooth fingertips create a light tapping sound, a replica of yesterday's cheek tapping. As if this isn't enough, like I'm not instantly aroused from the vision of his long fingers and the song they play, he adds the rings.

Yesterday's rings, I'm positive they are. They orchestrate a music that is a mixture of low thuds as they bump on the steering wheel and subtle clinks from clanking against each other.

Yesterday doesn't simply *return* to me. It barrels into my body, a heavy-duty jackhammer drilling a hole in my chest. At the last minute, I stifle a moan, biting the inside of my cheek until the pain takes over the intense, irrefutable arousal.

Unfortunately, biting my cheek isn't a foolproof plan against those damn fingers that hypnotize me.

The dampness between my thighs soaks through my panties, and my nipples poke through my bra. My thighs squeeze to relieve the pressure. Each breath is an effort.

It's made ten times worse by the steady hum of Callum to the words of the song. A catastrophe, really.

And then—as if I'm not weak enough at the knees as is—another force other than heat and pressure is aimed toward me. Callum's stare.

I don't see it. I feel it.

Neither of us wants this. We made it abundantly clear yesterday and today.

Neither of us can avoid it, either.

But I must. I force myself to think of Dad, of his disappointment, of his improvement that I can't afford to impede.

It's that little push to help me stop this madness. To revert to my old, willful self. To do what's right.

I turn my head to Callum the same time my hand locates the volume button on the electronic music panel. The man to my left returns the smirk I force on myself; his fingers continue tapping to this painful erotic tune.

My fingers clasp the volume button, about to spin it. "This is the kind of song you should play at full volume, or not at all."

Callum's lips part in a chuckle, one that my pussy and heart are saved from. The drums, guitar, and vocals to the song blast out through the car's surround system, and I turn my satisfied gaze to the road ahead.

I even let out a little sigh. I'm in the clear. For now.

CHAPTER EIGHT
Callum

Robin and I enter the lounge on the top floor, after being silent throughout the rest of the car ride. And as far as quiet times go, this isn't a bad one.

The void opened a portal for me, a chance to observe Robin closer than I have in the two years I've lived in Los Angeles.

She's grown up. Her gaze is more somber through her once-careless smiles. Her comebacks are Robin. Yet she's still very much attuned to me. As I am to her.

And I don't like how the arousal that seeped out of her every pore in the car has transformed into a reserved stance, a rigid walk. I don't question her about it. It's obvious why she'd be stressed.

I can't wait to put the little prick in his place.

We cross the marbled floors of the hallway to the two hostesses welcoming guests to the event, with my hand at Robin's back.

Her feet slow. I stop altogether, bowing to whisper to her, "Any last detail worth mentioning before we walk in?"

"Yes." Robin presses her cheek to mine.

Her scent carries to me, clean and citrusy. The scent of family trips and weekly dinners. The times spent together are a solid reminder of what I should be focusing on—her as a family member. A highly attractive, soft, and lush family member.

Easier said than done.

I still want to pull her body flush to me, still want to taste the mouth I shouldn't fantasize about. Still fucking crave to know how soft and supple it'll be around my cock.

I still do, and I need to stop it. I didn't ask to help her out so I could replace her harasser.

"We're a couple, one year, right?"

"Right," I grit out. My eyes are trained forward. If I look down at her body while her voice turns husky from whispering, I might as well throw my resolve in the trash.

"You can't say we met through…"

Her dad. "Wouldn't dream of it."

"Or the club."

Eva Marks

She's flustered, and cute. And I need to fucking quit thinking of her like that and focus on her.

"Robin, listen to my voice."

A man and a woman in a suit and a dress wave at her, staying at a distance seeing how she and I huddle and whisper. She waves back, her posture relaxing. Mine eases with her, seeing the guy over there isn't the asshole whose brain is way overdue for rewiring.

"Breathe in. Breathe out." It's hard to keep my voice level when her chest grazes my arm. "Focus. Tell me what it is you *do* want me to say. I'll sell it like it's the one and only truth."

"I'm not sure they'll ask." She spins her head slowly, looking me in the eye. The resolution and self-assuredness mesmerize and bind me to her. "In case they do, we met at our offices. You were going to meet a client and got the wrong floor—"

"I never get the wrong floor," I tease.

"—and got the wrong floor." Her voice is sharp, laced with a shy smile.

Back to… Nothing. Because there isn't an us. Not in the sense my head is going.

"I directed you to the law firm on the tenth floor, and—"

"Redmond-Schuller?"

"How did you know?"

"Went to school with Schuller, interned with Redmond." I pull back, creating some distance between us. "Great, then. The story is believable. One last thing, though."

"Yeah?"

I cross my arms, firm my stare. "You point the guy out to me."

Her shoulders hike up almost to her ears, her voice an urgent whisper. "No, please."

"I won't do anything to embarrass you." I glance to where Robin directs her new smile, to two older men in suits, waiting to talk until they walk inside. "I'll have a talk with him, that's all. About office ethics and keeping his hands off what's mine."

The word is blurted out easily. *Too* easily. Like it and Robin both belong in the world as one.

They don't.

Robin notices what I have. She blushes, her hand running to her hair.

I do what I'm paid to do for a living. Fix life using different phrasing. "I'm only acting like any other boyfriend would've. That way, asshole gets off your back, and I sleep better at night."

I'm about to lay out another persuading explanation when she's contemplating it for over a minute.

Then she says, "Okay. I will."

She's lying. There isn't a convincing bone in her acquiescence.

After a few seconds of my own inner debate, I drop the subject. I'm tuned in to people's expressions, and to hers more than the rest. I'll recognize him by myself.

"Let's go in."

Her lungs expand, gathering courage like I taught her. "Should we, uh, hold hands?"

I planned on resuming to rest my hand on her back, but then she had to go and offer that. The word *no* is being throttled by what I truly desire.

"Pretty sure that's what couples do."

"Yes, yes." Her eyes smile as a response to me. "They do."

I don't wait for her to take my open palm, sliding my fingers through hers, clasping our hands together. We move forward, past the hostesses and into the source of the music.

The *B&R Comp* annual party is impressive even by my standards. Our offices don't hold back at the annual Christmas parties we host at both branches, and *B&R*'s gives us a run for our money.

There are six food stands across the room. Behind each of them, a chef is working on any kind of imaginable finger-food—from sushi to Vernick fish, carpaccio, wagyu beef, and more I can't see from where we are standing.

A celebrity DJ plays a catchy Justin Timberlake song to a crowd of a few employees, under an elaborate set of blue and silver lights. They already look mildly intoxicated, and I don't blame them. Given the full bar equipped with expensive drinks they have on either side of the space, it's practically expected of them.

The interest in the high-party they set up wanes after I've done a quick once-over of the place back to Robin.

She sways her body to the sound, mouthing the words.

My smile can't be helped.

Nor can the heat she generates in my heart and groin.

We should eat. I'm not hungry—I'm searching for an excuse that'll relieve me of the hand holding since I can't seem to be a grown fucking man and do it myself.

I lower my lips to where she can hear me, careful not to brush them on her skin, as tempting as it is. "Want to grab something to eat?"

"Actually, I'm starving." Her smile broadens as she cranes her neck to look past her coworkers hoarding the lines next to each stand. "Maybe we could try the—"

"Robin." Her name is uttered in a sleazy, sexual way.

I hate that man automatically. The thump of his hand clasping at her back and Robin's instant rigidness pours fuel to my instant despise. My hand tightens on hers, emitting comfort.

On the inside, though, I'm livid.

Robin, indeed, doesn't need to point out to me who's the guy that's been harassing her.

That vile excuse for a human made himself known without even meaning to.

"Hands off." I direct my glare to him, tugging Robin so her body is pressed to mine.

He's got my full attention. He's going to wish he hasn't.

"Callum, it's fine," she hisses through clenched teeth.

The hell it is.

"Don't tell me that's your boyfriend."

My eyebrows lower on my forehead. "Don't tell me you're the guy who's been sexually harassing her."

"I haven't." He inches closer, visibly drunk. Too drunk. Not the funny, outgoing kind. The violent, blubbering kind. "Can't a guy compliment a girl anymore?"

"You can," I growl at him. "If you're being respectful about it. And even then, once is enough."

I wrap my arms around Robin, forcing her into a hug, pressing her to my chest. This isn't a pretense;

it's not an exhibition of what a fake boyfriend would do. Shielding her from him is downright primal.

"Go away, and stay away from her. Or any other woman who's not interested." I smirk, and it's an ugly one. "Though it's hard to picture anyone who would."

"I kinda thought she liked it." His shit-eating grin tells me Robin played no consenting part in his sick game. As if I needed additional proof other than her word.

"That's cute." Keeping my voice low, I take a step closer to him and seethe out words that are forbidden as they are the truth, "She has me. A real man who really loves *her*, the person, not just her beautiful face. Who actually cares about her and her feelings."

Robin gasps into my chest.

Yeah, can't believe these truths coming out of my mouth either. But here we are.

"About that," he starts slurring.

Jesus, this guy is an embarrassment.

His wobbling in place and my protective encasing of Robin harbor inquisitive stares. They try to pretend they're in deep conversation, but they're looking, all right.

"And about her fine—"

"Do *not* say what I think you're about to," I threaten in a low, menacing voice. "Not now, not fucking ever."

Robin clings to the lapels of my suit jacket, pulling on them.

"What, baby?" My tone turns into cotton candy for her.

Considering Dustin flat out admitted his harassment, my sudden tenderness is a goddamn miracle.

"Callum, I'm begging you."

The distress in her eyes is so potent, it's nearly alive. The creases on her forehead are ones I hope to never witness again years from now.

I'm the asshole who put them there, who contributed to the problem. And I'll be the asshole who fixes it. I stand behind my words from before. I care for her feelings, and I act on it.

"This'll be the last time he talks to you like that. Him or anyone else." My hand slides to cup the back of her neck, dragging her face to mine. "Because in a second, they'll all see who you belong to. And no one messes with what's mine."

My mouth closes in on hers. At first, we're just two bodies connected to each other. Her lips are soft, her scent swirls not around me, but inside me.

I'm overwhelmed.

Fucking overwhelmed.

Can't do anything except inhale her air into my lungs and press my forehead to hers.

She doesn't show signs of resistance, doesn't push me away. She does the opposite. Robin moans into my mouth. A low, sweet moan slipping into my soul and capturing my heart.

A surge of emotion I've been bottling up for over two years thrashes against my chest. I pull her in an attempt to mold our bodies into one. My fingers dig into her hair; her fingers crumple my shirt.

I coax her lips open, groaning at the taste of her sweet tongue as she twists into mine. We explore each other, playing, growing hungrier by the second.

My cock is hard, painful, in a need to be inside her. I wrap a hand around the small of her back, grinding her soft belly to my throbbing length.

Two years of pining for the forbidden fruit and one insane session where I couldn't touch her at the club, culminated into an explosion.

Over nine hundred days where I fought hard against keeping my dick in my pants and my heart locked from the power she exerts on it. She's funny, kind. The part of me I haven't realized I've been missing. I wanted all of it for myself.

And I can't have her.

The seeds of how ethically and logically and morally corrupt wanting her is, they remain sowed within me. They're a reminder. She isn't mine to take.

She's my best friend's daughter.

But for fuck's sake, I can't stop myself.

Kissing her, touching her, roaming my hand on every inch of her skull. I lay claim to her, if only for tonight, only for this moment.

"Robin," I whisper, my conscience pulling me away from her lips.

I let my eyes flutter shut, tuning myself to the sound of her heavy breathing. They carry me to our night at *Into the Night*, to how *mine* she was back then.

I open my eyes to her swollen lips, clear of her lipstick. I run my thumb on the length of her bottom lip, gazing at her eyes. They speak words and promises, same as I'm aching to give her. Longings and vows neither of us can afford to utter.

A groan, Dustin's I assume, reaches my ears. I remember why I'm there, why I'm kissing her and making this scene. My head snaps up, searching for him. His back is to us; his sloppy feet carry him to the other side of the loft.

"Oh my God." Robin's forehead presses to my chest, her fingernails scratching my chest above my shirt. "I can't believe we made a scene. Fuck. Everyone's looking, aren't they?"

"No, baby." I brush her hair, knowing it's the last time. I won't get a repeat at that. "Even Dustin is gone. For good, I hope. You're safe."

"Thank you," she mumbles to the hollow place where my heart is.

"I'm sorry it had to be this way." The slow strokes of her soft locks are treasured and locked into memory. "It won't happen again. You have my word."

"What if I…"

"Don't. Please. We can't." I draw her back by the shoulders, leveling my eyes with hers. "Let's enjoy the rest of the night? Focus on that?"

She opens her mouth, then closes it. The second time she opens it, words and confidence stream out. "Yeah, okay. Can we meet my teammates?"

I smile, even though the sinking feeling refuses to release its hold on me. "After you."

CHAPTER NINE
Callum

I want to kiss her again.

I want to kiss Robin at sunrise, before my legs burn from running ten miles through the streets of New York.

I want to kiss her in the early morning. In the shower where I wash the workout off, while shaving my face and styling my hair.

I want to kiss her on the bike ride to work. Want it so fucking bad I can feel her lips from three days ago. I still fucking want it.

I. Want. Her.

My need for her doesn't take the backseat throughout the day. Doesn't get better at the office.

It's crucial that I focus on the case I'm representing, on Ron, the client who has been wrongly accused of murdering his mother. Garland handed me invaluable evidence pointing to Ron's sister, and it's my job to piece the story together for the jury to clear Ron.

Witness questioning needs to be lined up, court arrangements to be prepped in advance. Each word I'll utter out of my mouth in front of the jury matters. The task is the team's and mine to carry out, through meetings, evidence study, and old cases to back up our case.

Our client is counting on us.

And I can't fucking get Robin out of my head.

Her lips, the sound of her moans. Her hitched breaths and the hammering of her heart.

Most people experience a range of emotions when they listen to music. Joy or a heartache, ecstatic to the point they just *have* to dance or so morose they lie in bed while the song plays on every last one of their heartstrings.

The song Robin's body played for me, it does all of that and more.

It makes me hard.

It has me fantasizing about what I shouldn't. To hold and love her in the most intimate, cherishing, and inappropriate ways.

My guilt, akin to my needs, intensifies as minutes pass.

And then it's everywhere, when, after two long months, her dad finally calls.

Eva Marks

His name is a warning sign flashing on my phone. My heart drops. I've been waiting for his call, moved to another state to be there when it happened so I can be at his place at a moment's notice.

But is it the call I've been looking for?

Is it possible he knows?

"Wes, man."

I summon my lawyer's voice upon answering. It's stern to show the jury how fucking confident I am, yet not too stern at the same time, because otherwise I'm just another stuck-up lawyer who'll defend even the worst of humanity as long as the money rolls in.

And the main reason I use it with my best friend today out of all days? To hide what I'm feelings inside. And that's a lot.

"Hi, Callum." It's not his usual self, per se, though nothing to indicate a broken-down man. I sigh internally with relief.

"How have you been?"

I can imagine damn well how, but I'm not about to go all passive aggressive on him. I stand behind what I told Robin—he deserves a break. A bunch of them.

"Listen, I want to apologize for not picking up. I've been a jerk. I'm sorry."

"I'm not accepting it." Not when I'm the one who should be begging for his forgiveness. I spin my chair to face the west side of the city. "There's nothing you need to apologize for. Absolutely nothing."

Somewhere in the view out of my office is Wes's home. My best friend. The one I can't disappoint by taking one of the two most precious treasures he has left.

"There is. There's a lot of it. Maggie being gone…" He's defeated, and I can't fucking take it. "It's not an excuse not to shut you out."

"Doesn't change my opinion. Not accepting it."

He lets out a short laugh. He's better. He's on the path to healing.

And I want to haul his daughter up in her room and kiss every inch of her skin. Her lips. Her breasts. To get lost in her cunt for days.

Some best friend I am.

"You've always been a stubborn bastard."

"Only for what my conscience is bound to." I get up, striding to the floor-to-ceiling window. New York's skies are clear, the spring's sun thawing off the last remains of the winter.

They do nothing to placate my lying heart when I add, "Family, and the truth."

The two concepts that were set in stone less than a week ago are now crumbling. But, for the sake of keeping my chosen family in one piece, I press pause on the truth part.

"Yeah." Wes clears his throat.

It's hard to recognize him in his weakened state, and it steels my resolve to not ever tell him about Robin or pursue her further. I owe him to be better, at least until he's fully himself again.

"So, anyway," he says. "You still in the city?"

"Yeah." A smile creeps on my lips, thinking about Robin. "The yellow taxis, monster high-rises, and endless foot traffic. I'm in the dead center of it."

"You forgot about the Knicks."

Ah. There's my friend.

"Just because I can't forget about the Lakers."

His laugh is real this time. "Definitely a stubborn bastard. So, I was thinking…"

The hesitation returns to his voice. He contemplates whether I'll tell him to fuck off after screening my calls for two months or not. I'm not having that.

"My place is open twenty-four seven for you. In fact, I cleared it with my building's concierge to give you keys and let you come up whenever you want. You don't even have to call before you come. If you're in the neighborhood or whatever, feel free to drop by. Anytime."

"I'm taking you up on the offer to get together, but forget me dropping by unannounced. Barging in on your naked ass having sex in college was enough to last me a lifetime."

He's not wrong. I had my share of meaningless sex. Twenty-five years ago. Today, after releasing the demon I kept locked inside, I'm after one girl and one girl only. I won't go looking for another woman, won't return to *Into the Night*.

The one woman I *do* want is off-limits. There's no reason for him not to drop by. That's what I'm here for, after all.

"Nah, I'm taking a break." It's not an actual lie. There's nothing out there for me. "Worst thing is you open the door to a crime series, blood and guts and someone storing body parts in the fridge."

"I'm not sure which is worse," he shoots back. It's a part of our banter. A part of the old him that he passed on to Robin.

"You'll have to tell me when you do come, then."

"Will do."

"Great." The clinking heels of Mabel forces me to cut the call short. "I have to get back to work. I'll be seeing you?"

"About that."

I stop mid-turn to my secretary, frozen in place. *He doesn't know. He can't.*

"I'm having a late lunch this Saturday afternoon, inviting the girls over. I was hoping you could join us, you know, just close family."

Eva Marks

The D9 bulldozer doesn't ease off its pressure on my chest. On one hand, I'll get to see Wes after two months of being worried sick about him.

On the other hand, I'll be seeing his daughter.

I'm not one-hundred percent able to manage having both in the same room, but I have no choice. I'll have to find it within me, will have to put up my court appearance front and give the performance of a lifetime.

My best friend can't and won't know that I want his daughter. That I had my tongue inside her mouth and my hands on her body.

He can't and he won't.

"I'd love that." I accept the folder Mabel hands me, sliding into my leather chair. "Say the word and I'm there."

CHAPTER TEN
Robin

"Adele, pass me the salad bowl." I balance two soda bottles in the crook of my left arm and a salt shaker in my palm.

Dad invited the both of us in our group chat to late Saturday lunch, like he did *before*. Neither of us could've said no to that. School, work, friends, they were pushed to the side for us to spend a few hours here and make our father happy.

When I hugged Dad as I walked in, my heart stung in an unpleasant way. I feel horrible about keeping this Callum monster-sized secret from him. Nervous, too. It's like every time he looks at me, I feel like he *knows* I did something.

Eva Marks

I have to remind myself over and over how impossible it is. I'm not supposed to know Callum is here.

And smile.

Adele takes a break from dumping the noodles and sushi from the takeout containers into plates. She looks at me, her head shaking watching my poor balancing skills. But that doesn't stop her from helping me steady the salad bowl on my right palm so it'll rest on my belly instead of crashing to the floor.

"Always the overachiever."

"That's not being an overachiever, it's just common sense. Like I told you a million times, sis." I blow on a strand of hair that covers my eye. "If I don't have to walk back and forth more than once, you can bet I won't do it."

She raises an eyebrow, her lips quirking into a smirk. "You're one lazy New Yorker, you know that?"

The condensation on the soda bottles drips. They start slipping on my arms. I poke my tongue out at Adele, then head toward the doors on the other side of the kitchen.

Some six or seven years ago, when Maggie was still Mom and not some evil stranger, she had the kitchen be a separate part of the house. She hated how the cooking scents overrode her precious

DAD *can't* KNOW

Chanel No. 5 and strongly disliked the clatter of pots and pans while she and her friends were sipping on champagne and gossiping about whomever.

She hasn't always been like this. Mom, in our past life as I call it now, was sweet and fun. Hugging and caring. She and Dad snuggled on the couch on snowy weekends, and she'd make hot cocoa for Adele and me without us ever having to ask.

That's probably why her slow changes didn't raise any red flags that something was wrong. Why all of this took us by such a fucking surprise.

Oh well, maybe I can convince Dad to remodel sometime.

With my back to Adele, I say, "I'd rather walk a hundred miles forward than back and forth like a yo-yo."

She tsks and chuckles behind me. It's peaceful. Almost normal. Mom might not be here, but it doesn't make us any less of a family. Fuck her. We'll reclaim our happiness with or without her.

I'm setting the bowl and drinks on our living room table, keeping it super casual and homey like we used to. Dad's upstairs, finishing up a business call to Europe, and I want everything to be perfect and ready for him once he's finished.

The bottles are placed over coasters, the salt shaker and salad put strategically in the center of the table.

Clink.

A key turns in Dad's front door lock.

Whoosh.

The heavy metal door to the apartment slides across the floor.

The energy in the room transforms into something heavy. The kitchen is almost hermetically closed, leaving me with the sounds of a familiar set of shoes clicking on our marble floors.

My back is to the front door, my eyes fixed ardently on Central Park. I don't want to look elsewhere, to face *him*. Callum is here, I can sense it.

Though he shouldn't be.

Dad said only family. Family, for the last two months, has been the three of us.

But of course, he's family. Of course, he'll be here seeing Dad's mood start picking up. He moved here for this exact reason.

He wouldn't pass on a family lunch just because we…

We…

What is so bad about what we did, exactly?

We had an incredible ASMR sex. A one-off thing. A mistake we'll never repeat.

Then he kissed me for the sake of getting Dustin to stop harassing me, since I didn't allow Callum to make a scene. Another occurrence that wouldn't happen ever again.

So…since both were singular accidents that would never happen again, then nothing's really changed between us. We were Uncle Callum and Robin, same as we've always been.

Except… my heart.

Sigh.

"Robin." The warm touch of his hand lands on my shoulder.

Stress has taken my head hostage, and I didn't hear him taking the rest of the steps behind me.

I scream.

"Shh." Callum's thumb massages me through my dress. "It's me."

My eyes slant to my side where he stands. I notice he's wearing a black T-shirt stretching across his taut chest, and blue jeans that hang low on his sculpted hips. Comfy, like me in my simple, off-white T-shirt dress.

I almost laugh at how different we are today compared to the last two times I saw him last week.

Almost, yet I don't. Our situation isn't funny in the slightest. Me wanting to repeat our kiss doesn't amuse me. The pull at my center is the farthest thing from a knock-knock joke.

But I get my shit together. He's here. I'm here. Dad and Adele could walk through the doors any second now. They'll see something's wrong if I'm silent like I have a sock shoved down my throat.

"Breathe in. Breathe out."

It's both annoying and comforting how he knows what to say and what intonation to use to get to me. It makes me forget the million layers of embarrassment I should be feeling for my reaction to him.

My heart rate slows, eventually. I'm calm, composed, and able to search for his face.

"Hey." Callum isn't confused. Isn't baffled.

So composed.

Unlike me.

The lines at the corners of his eyes deepen, and he smiles.

Again, I'm not that entertained, not upset though, either.

I'm unsettled. I crave his touch under the roof where I most certainly shouldn't. I'm magnetized to him when my sister is in the kitchen. My dad could be here any second now.

The dissonance kills me. I'm torn. Ripped and wanting.

Callum's hand drops to the side at my confused stare. "Everything okay?"

No. "Yes."

"Positive about that?" His smooth forehead creases, his attorney eyes launching into a cross examination as they dip into my soul. "That Dustin guy still harassing you?"

Dustin. That's an easy enough topic to focus on. "No. What you did…"

I let the words hang between us. I'm referring to more than the accusations and borderline threats Callum made to Dustin's face. I'm talking about the kiss, hoping to find the arousal I saw in him the other day.

Callum doesn't smile anymore. His stoic expression doesn't let on whether the memory does anything to him one way or another.

"Anyway." Disappointed and relieved, I brush it off, putting my guard up.

I can't handle the calamity of emotions inside my body. It'll end up driving me insane. "It helped. Dirty Dustin hasn't come on to me or around me the entire week. Haven't seen him lurking around other women, so that's always a plus."

"It is."

"Uncle Callum!"

Thank fucking fuck for Adele. She speed-walks to where we're standing, throws empty plates and cutlery on the table, and wraps her arms around him. "When did you get here? Dad didn't tell us you were coming."

"Dad said it was a *family* lunch." My father jogs down the stairs in plain jeans and a T-shirt. His cheeks are less hollow than they were two weeks ago, and there's lightness to his movements. "Callum is family."

He and Callum hug each other, and I pull on Adele's arm to get her to come with me and give them some space. Five minutes later, after my sister reiterates my thoughts and tells me what a great sign it is that Dad called Uncle Cal, we return, carrying our microwave heated plates.

Callum sits down on the armchair, by himself. The three of us sit on the sofa next to Dad with Adele on the edge closest to him, Dad in the middle, and me on the other, safer side.

The distance isn't sufficient to keep my hormones in check, but it's something.

Across from here his cologne is fainter and his flexing muscles as he brings food to his mouth are hidden by my family. I can semi-focus on my chewing, on giving the rest of my attention to Adele's stories about college life and to Dad saying he hopes she doesn't think about a permanent move.

What I cannot overcome through the distance, though, are the sound of his rings meeting the top of the table.

At first, I think it's a mistake. He puts his plate down, reaches for his glass, and they scrape the table. It surprises me, morphs the dullness of my need for him into a sharp, impaling craving. Which I force down.

I got this under control.

No biggie.

Callum keeps engaging in the conversation with Adele and Dad. For a minute there, I really do buy into the lie I told myself about this being an accident.

"I remember freshman year." *Clink, clink, clink,* Callum's rings go on his glass. "I was so out of it." *Clink.* "If it weren't for your dad, I wouldn't have made it through the first semester."

The handle of the fork I'm holding digs into my skin. My eyes are honed in on the food, though I can't really see anything. Callum pushes my buttons repeatedly, and I'm helpless against the surge of lust that follows.

"Give me a break. I had more alcohol tolerance than you, that's all."

Dad's voice serves as a reprieve from Callum's torture and as a vehement reminder; I. Cannot. Be. Thinking. These. Thoughts.

He can't be doing this intentionally. People's fingers drum. It's a thing. It happens. They have a song stuck in their head, they tap their fingers to it.

"Girls, forget I said that." Dad turns from Adele to me, smiling. "Too much alcohol is bad for you."

Remember that smile. Remember how you don't want to take it from him.

"Plus, it's illegal." Callum's smugness doesn't evade me. Like the cocky man I met at the club.

Stop thinking with your vagina! Dad's literally an inch away!

Reaching for my own glass, I down the remaining soda in two gulps. Refreshing.

Better.

"Robin," Callum says in a deep voice. I stifle a moan, barely. "Can you pass me the soda?"

My cough is a direct result of what my horny brain hears.

Can you give me a blowjob?

For fucking fuck's sake.

I pass him the bottle, avoiding any finger contact, and stand up. "Everyone finished?"

"Why the rush?" Dad cranes his neck up. "I know your sister has to go soon. You too?"

"Yeah. Lots of papers. The usual." The lie comes easily when I'm staring at Dad's knee. My hair falls down my cheeks, so I'm pretty sure the resulting blush would be hidden as well. "And actual work. You know. The usual."

"Okay, then." Dad pats my arm. His tender tone sends me on a guilt trip straight to hell.

It sucks to leave him this early. I studied late last night then squeezed in a few hours this morning to be able to have another hour or two here. Maybe someday when my body isn't reeling from kissing Callum a week ago.

"Don't let your old man keep you."

Humiliation piles up on my guilt. An abundance of it, seeing I'm falling—or more accurately, fell—for a man as old as my father.

"You're not old, Dad," I say more to myself than to him.

"Yeah, yeah." He gets up to help me.

I push him down. "I'm on it. You need your strength."

Dad's gray eyes gaze up at mine, glimmering with emotion. "I must have done something right to be so lucky to have the two of you girls."

That's all I can take for today. I rush to stack the empty plates of the four of us. My trembling hands are to blame for their slight clinking. I pile on the forks and knives, making a beeline to the kitchen.

I hear more clinking, then footsteps behind me. It's probably my wishful thinking. I told them I had this; no one should be following me. My arm presses on the door to the kitchen.

But I never have the time to allow my body weight to push it in.

Rings clink as they meet the door's surface, and the fragrance of his virile cologne curls around me.

"Let me help."

CHAPTER ELEVEN
Callum

I tried. I really did.

I haven't turned my gaze from Wes and Adele throughout the entire lunch, focusing on them instead of on the temptation to their left.

I listed a million reasons why going after Robin was the worst fucking idea of my life.

And this right here is why I hate myself more. Sitting here in their company, I know I don't need a million reasons.

I don't need so much as two.

I need one, and one alone—she's my best friend's daughter.

There's no precedence to this. None of our friends or acquaintances had anything remotely similar happening to them. This should be an easy choice. Wes is fine, or will be very soon. I'll move back to Los Angeles, leave the girl alone, and find someone my own goddamn age.

Case open, case shut.

Only it isn't. Even I don't believe the bullshit I'm feeding myself.

With Robin near me, so close I can reach out and touch her, I realize I can't walk away. Her adorable little smile, the hint of her sass she gives her sister, and fuck, the outline of her breasts as well—I can't imagine a life without it.

Can't hold on to the promise I haven't spoken but am bound to anyway: Thou shalt not fall for thy best friend's daughter.

Or think about coming inside her every hour of every fucking day.

"I can handle a few plates," Robin says to the floor, denying my help.

Denying her at the party might have hurt her. It's either that, or she's embarrassed by me showing up here. Possibly both.

And I know just how to make it right.

"You don't have to, though." I trail behind her into the kitchen, closing the door behind me and barricading us inside.

The light switch is automated, bathing the kitchen in a warm glow. It gives Robin's hair a golden hue, softening her already delicate features.

"I can help you with other things, Robin." My voice drops an octave as I lean into the counter. "Can help the both of us."

She shivers, the plates nearly tumbling out of her hands to the floor. I wipe out the distance between her and me in two long strides.

I'm next to her, gripping her hand and looking into her eyes.

"Don't." She holds my gaze in hers. "I need a minute. I need to wash these dishes."

"Need a hand?"

"Need to think."

She's so expressive, her emotions spill out of her in waves. I recognize them because they're identical to mine. To be a decent and honorable person for Wes's sake versus adhering to the inner voice that tells me this is a once-in-a-lifetime opportunity.

To not let her slip through my fingers.

"Callum." She sighs. "My thoughts scare me."

"Wash the dishes then, please." I take a step back, gesturing at the water. "The sound of the water will soothe you."

Her cute nose wrinkles, and she goes at it.

I'm quiet while I observe her surrendering herself to the calm the simple action gives her. She's beautiful.

No. She isn't. Calling her *beautiful* is an insult to what she really is. She's wonderful. The whole package. The certainty of never finding someone remotely close to Robin is overwhelming, more final than even a death penalty.

I have to get her to see it too, free of fear.

We have to at least give it a chance, start somewhere. The other parts will fall into place. I'll make sure of it.

I would've told her all of it in great detail. Thing is, she doesn't seem to be in the mood to talk. Her serenity transforms into stress at one point, and she scrubs those dishes like her family doesn't own a dishwasher to wipe them clean for her.

Her face is scrunched, her shoulders hiked up.

There's one way I know how to pull her out of it, to have her hear me out.

"Robin." I step toward her, my chest grazing her arm.

"I'm still thinking." Her resigned voice is the opposite of the violent rubs of the plate at her hand.

"I don't want to talk." My whole body works in unison to restrain myself from lowering my teeth to her neck, to evoke a gasp out of her.

"Okay."

"I do need something to help you through your thinking process."

"Please don't let Dad catch us." The verbal explanation confirms what I've been picking up on from her. That's why being in the same room with me turns her into a flustered, beautiful mess.

"I won't. I have good hearing, in case anyone will come near here. I'll know ten steps ahead." My hand strokes along her slim waist, shifting the sleeve of her dress up as I move. "You trusted me your whole life. You can trust me now."

She releases one hand from the plate, grasping at the counter. The rest of her body turns still. The water continues to gush over a sparkling clean plate she holds up to them.

"I do." Her breaths are heavy, her words clipped.

"I want more from you." I roll my rings along the counter. Sounds of metal sliding on marble fill the air.

Robin's lips press together, a choked moan fighting against its prison.

"Do you want to be mine, baby?"

It's this not the first time the term of endearment leaves my lips around Robin. I always considered it the mother of all clichés. But if the shoe fits... And fuck, how it does with her.

"Dad." She sighs, lowering the plate to the sink. "It'll tear him apart."

"It'll be okay. I'll make Wes see reason," I say, willing to stand behind my vow through thick and thin. "Any roadblock life will put ahead of us, I'll demolish it."

Her desperate eyes slither into my soul, wanting to believe me. "Dad's not a roadblock."

"He isn't. Dealing with it will be." My body and voice exude confidence and love, for her and her dad alike. "I swear to you I'll fix it. You and I, we're not a sin. He'll understand."

"I want you, just not—"

I graze the curve of her spine. She gives me a gasp.

It isn't the one I remember from the club. There's a deeper level of emotion to it. And I'm the greedy fuck who wants more of it.

Two of my fingers land between her parted lips, pressing down her tongue. "Open wide."

She does, allowing me to push them forward, drift them down her mouth. They hit the back of her throat. Her eyes tear up, then she gags at the intrusion.

My jaw stills, my muscles tense at the erotic sound.

"Stay there." I pull my fingers out abruptly, moving to stand behind her.

Both my hands lock her in on each side; my body is flush against her back. Using my knees, I shove the back of hers to the cupboards until they're pressed up against it.

The first thing I do is hum in her ear. A gentle, low, monotone vibration while tapping one finger to her navel.

"I can't get you out of my head, Robin."

"Callum, they'll hear," she whispers a warning that contrasts the encouraging arch of her ass to me.

I thrust her forward. "Back to the counter."

Thump.

A single sound can evoke a world of feelings. For me, in this minute, with this thump, it's the awakening of the beast. It's her cunt hitting the cabinet. It's her clit getting the attention it must be starving for.

And I'm going to hear it again.

My hips dry hump her ass, my erection sliding along the crease between her butt cheeks.

"Close your eyes, Robi, and listen to the sounds your body creates." I grab a fistful of the side of her ass, growling against her skin. "Does getting your pussy pounded on the cabinet feels as good as listening to it?"

"Yes," she mouths, adding a million yeses after that.

Suddenly, I become aware that using sounds alone might make her lost in a fantasy, rather than concentrate on *us*.

I want her to remember it's me she's craving after she comes. At work, while she studies.

I want my face to haunt her in her dreams.
"Look at me."
She doesn't show a sign of hesitation, whipping her head back and opening her eyes wide. She's turned on, but not lost in any way.

She's alive and right here with me.

"I bet your pretty dripping cunt ruined your panties."

I don't wait for her confirmation, tilting my hips back to shove a hand under her dress and her panties to the side. Three fingers are rammed into her pussy at once.

The sexiest sound I've ever heard of my fingers in her pussy echoes in the kitchen, accompanied by the feel of her tight walls and sweet, decadent warmth.

Robin clenches around me. Gasps for me. Grinds her ass back, for me.

All of it is for me.

"You missed me, didn't you?"

Her pleading gaze ensnares mine. "I-I…"

"Don't be shy, Robin. I have no problem admitting I missed you." I slip my thumb back to stroke her pucker, wetting it with her juices and probing into her tight hole.

Our foreheads are pressed together, breathing each other's air.

Eva Marks

"Did you miss me? Missed how I made your pussy feel better?"

"Yeah."

Without leaving her, I bend forward to grab a wineglass off the rack, laying it on top of the counter.

"Suck these for me." I bury my fingers inside her mouth again. "Coat them in spit, I'm gonna need them wet."

She complies, covering my fingers in her saliva. Her body and her eyes are a ball of unspent energy as she expects my next move.

I slide my fingers on the rim of the glass, swirling it around the edge. Robin's response is immediate; her lips are pressed into a white line, her arousal consuming her from the inside out.

"You like that, don't you?" My fingers are back to her pussy, fucking her relentlessly. I lose interest in the glass, pulling my hand from it to force Robin's face to mine. "Like having my attention. Like making me hard."

A sharp breath fills her lungs, and for a moment, I'm lost in her.

In the maddening state I'm in, I couldn't give a flying fuck whether we are caught like this by the Chief Justice of the Supreme Court. The need to have her and listen to her come in an ear-piercing scream are the only two truths of my existence.

But I force myself to know better. I promised her everything will be okay, and I will not break my promises.

"You're gonna come soon." Releasing her jaw, I reach back to get a dishtowel. "And you'll want to scream. That's why"—I stuff her mouth with it—"you're gonna suck on this."

Her watery eyes produce two silent tears. The towel didn't bring this on. My fourth finger in her pussy as I pin her to the cabinets does.

"Next time I'll be telling you to suck on something, it won't be a dishtowel." I lean close to her face, my breath fanning at her cheek. "And, baby, you'll look so beautiful choking on my cock."

I use my spit-wet fingers to rub her clit as fast as the fingers of my other hand pleasure her ass and pussy. She's being pounded and served everywhere.

"Now, come."

When my lips suck on her jaw, she finally gives in. Robin comes, and it's the mother of all spectacles.

"Baby." I whip out the towel, bringing her to me, and kiss her lips.

She kisses me back with what little strength she has left, clinging to my sides.

I would prolong the moment, except there's someone nearing us. Footsteps stalk toward the kitchen, and I step back, quickly smoothing over Robin's hair and dress.

Her eyes narrow in question, until she hears her sister too.

"Robin? What's taking you forever?"

CHAPTER TWELVE
Robin

"Come home with me."

Callum's whisper descends into my accepting ears even from the distance he's put between us.

I crave it but…

What have we gotten ourselves into?

This isn't a mistake anymore.

He came at me; he started it.

He *wants* me. I want him back, a lot. In my dad's house, while he's in the adjacent room.

That's how bad I want Callum. I'm willing to risk Dad having a relapse just so I can have his best friend.

It's reckless. It's selfish. It's horrible. It's everything I promised I wouldn't do to Dad the last time I vowed to never hurt him again.

Eva Marks

And still, the agony of longing for Callum suffocates me. I'm attracted to him, have been for years. I'm also in love with him, I can admit to it now.

But maybe there is a way I can stop this insanity. Maybe he asked me to come home with him so I could return the favor, be a good little fuck toy to be tossed aside later. If this is the situation, if he says it to my face, I can walk away.

Getting nothing from him is better than to keep pounding at the door of his unattainable heart.

He's an honest man, and he wouldn't lead me on. All I have to do is ask.

"Why?"

Callum's gaze flickers to the wall, hinting to my sister approaching.

I put my hands on my hips, demanding in a harsh whisper, "Tell me why."

"I want you." Acting against his words, he steps back.

"What for?"

"Robin."

His stern expression does nothing to deter me. "We would've been done with this conversation if you would've answered a minute ago."

"To spend the night together." He sees me opening my mouth, ready to stop him and deny what he's asking of me. "Doing anything. It may come off as fucking desperate, but fuck it, I don't give a shit. I want you in my apartment, and I'll take anything you'll give me. Watch movies, talk, have sex, hug you without hiding. That's why."

The rest of my resolve and loyalty to my father's betterment explode and flail like ashes of a burnt paper to the floor.

The last thing he said returns to haunt me. "We *will* be hiding, though."

He grips the counter. "Robin."

"Uncle Callum." Adele pushes the kitchen's door and waltzes in. "Robin, come on. I have the drive to Jersey and a shit ton of studies after I give you a ride home."

"Don't worry about it." Callum's face is serene and in control. His voice is smooth, his stance relaxed against the counter. Just another family gathering. "I'll drive her. It's faster on my bike."

Adele disturbs her bottom lip, glancing between us. Panic grips at my lungs like a vise. Did we forget anything? Does his bite mark show? Does the room smell of sex?

What am I going to do if she notices?

Fuck, fuck, fuck.

"And more dangerous."

The groan in my throat is stifled. Fuck. Of course, that's what bothers her. We practically lost our mother. Losing another family member.

"She'll have my second helmet on." Callum walks toward Adele—this shameless, sexy man—and places the hand that hadn't been inside my pussy on her arm. "She'll be safe with me. Always has been, always will be."

He addresses both Adele and me alike, sending a different message to each of us. His intonation slithers into my soul, turning the temperature of my body from cozy warm into sizzling hot.

There's something to be said about his intonation and honorable character. They capsize my original hopes for a movie night and long talks over tea and cake. My clit is a pressure point between my thighs, and my lungs fill with unimaginable desire.

I'm turned on by his respect for me. The need is undeniable, and I need to do something about it.

As in, yesterday.

"It's not like I don't ride my own bike." I snap out of my stupor.

"Doesn't mean I like it."

Callum turns to me, but I don't look at him. One meaningful gaze in front of my sister risks *everything*.

"I think I lost something." Scratching my chin, I glance up to the ceiling. I lift my finger in the air, looking back to Adele. "Oh, yes. It's my last fuck."

Feeling Callum's smirk, the warmth of it, is all but fucking divine.

"You're a dick." She shakes her head, huffing a laugh.

"Sorry, Deli, without my poor fucking fuck, I have no other choice." I prance past her and to the kitchen door. "Uncle Call's bike it is."

His footsteps and hers follow me. Dad has his arm sprawled on the back of the sofa, head twisted to the three of us. I make it to him first, rubbing his shoulder affectionately at a safe distance.

Callum's cologne lingers on my skin. I can't risk it.

"I'm gonna go too, Dad. Uncle Callum will drop me off at the apartment."

He stands up. "You sure?"

Adele's groan starts from behind me, then at my side. That's a long groan, a theatrical, funny one. "You don't stand a chance, Dad. Missy here lost all her *fucking fucks*."

"Girls!" he yells through his laughter, signaling with his chin to Callum who still stands at a distance.

I look at him over my shoulder while Adele says something to Dad.

Then I show myself just how true Adele's statement is.

I wink at him.

Eva Marks

My sister joins us on the ride down the elevators, her silver Porsche Spyder right behind us on the way out of the parking lot.

Saying I have zero fucks to give turns out to be a blatant lie. Callum and I are, after all, being chaperoned by Adele. I avoided his blue gaze at the elevators, and now, sitting on his bike, you'd think he has some infectious disease the way I hardly grip his waist.

Though it isn't a disease I'm scared of. He's given me his leather jacket, so nothing separates us other than the two thin fabrics of clothes. Leaning another inch on him would result in me melting into him, blowing our cover altogether.

For Adele to see in broad daylight.

Nope. Not in this lifetime, or the next.

"I promised your sister I'll keep you safe," Callum says through the mic inside the helmet, sounding amused.

I release one hand, tugging my dress lower. "What about us not getting caught?"

The gates to the street slide open slowly. My body simmers at the idea of being alone with him and not having to worry about anything and anyone. To just be his.

Foot traffic appears on the street. We're about to get out.

"The first turn I take on the street, you'll fall. Holding on to me is the rational thing to do. You, Adele, and I know it."

"She hasn't ridden before."

"Trust me, the way she stressed out over you up there, I'm sure she's yelling in her car for you to hold me tighter, not the opposite." Smugness filters through his tone.

Yeah, right, Adele's mental state is his primary concern.

I respect him enough to agree to anything he says. But this game he's playing? I can play it harder.

"I agree." My arms engulf him, my chest pressed to his wide, hard back. "Adele shouldn't have to suffer through anxiety on her ride to college."

We drive out of the parking lot, veering to the left in the direction of my apartment. Callum blends into traffic gracefully. He won't be so graceful soon.

"Speaking of my sister." My hand drifts down his stomach to the top of his jeans.

"Careful, now."

"Do you think she saw how hard you were for me?" I'm fingering his top button, my voice thick with lust. "I mean, I didn't look, but I felt your cock.

And you're big, Uncle Callum. She only had to glimpse down to get a view of it."

"Robi, I'm warning you."

We pass one green light after the other. The nonstop drive is probably what saves me from having his hand rip mine off when it slides lower to cup his erection.

I moan. It's partly fake. Mostly it isn't. That man's erection is thick in my palm, swelling on my one long stroke back up to the tip.

"Looking to get arrested for public indecency?"

He's doing everything in his power to remain calm and somewhat menacing. It's no use. The power is in my hands, literally.

"I have a good lawyer."

Stroke.

His muscles tense beneath me, and he curses.

Callum's filthy mouth is hot. That hot, that I continue to poke him to get more of it.

"Will it fit?" I slip a hand under his shirt, inserting my thumb between the waistband of his jeans and his stomach. "Inside me? I was only with one person, and it was over a year ago."

"Stop. It."

We turn into my neighborhood, and he slows down. He won't leave me here, but he might pull over and have the upper hand. I have to be quick.

"I must be so, so very tight, Uncle Callum." His strong thighs clench as my palm massages his balls. "Will you be gentle?"—*moan*—"Or will you rip me open in one shove?"

"I said, stop it."

The bike slows on our ride through the East Village streets. Callum raises his hand, and I apply more pressure on his dick to stop him from prying mine off him.

Except he doesn't go there. He raps his rings on his helmet.

My confident touch falters, and I moan for the third time. A real moan, unfiltered and unstoppable.

"To your question." His hand returns to the bike's handle. "I'm going to own your tight little hole. You've been bad, really fucking bad. I planned on kissing your pussy, sucking your clit. You would've come so hard your muscles would've relaxed and you'd be dripping wet on my sheets, ready for my size to fill you up. Now, I'm leaning toward pinning your knees to either side of you, spitting on your cunt and fucking you so hard the bed breaks."

Our little charade of driving me, quote-unquote, home is over. He's spinning the bike back up through vast intersections.

"You're gonna take me raw?" I sigh.

His cock jerks in my palm. "I'll take you however I like, and you'll thank your Uncle Callum for it, Robin."

"M-hmm."

"And you'll behave." The bike slows at a stop sign. Callum takes my hand, returning it to his stomach.

I pretend to be on my best behavior until he starts driving again.

Then I start rocking my hips.

"I said behave." His grunt reverberates through the speakers, hardening my nipples in a sweet kind of torture.

"I can't, Uncle Callum," I purr. "My empty pussy is sopping, and the wind blowing on it is making me so, so horny."

My hand strokes him without an ounce of shame.

"Fuck." He groans, then shoots back, "I'll be balls deep inside you like you wanted, orchestrating a whole fucking symphony out of slapping your tits."

I ignore him, too turned on to stop this game. "I'm hurting, Uncle Callum, I'm hurting and I'm horny. I'm grinding behind you, can you feel me fucking your bike seat?"

"I won't wear a condom, to your other question." He swerves the bike to the sidewalk and into a storage space building. "I'm clean, and I'm taking you. Now."

CHAPTER THIRTEEN
Callum

I pull up to one of the roller doors, pressing on the remote to open the gate to my unit.

Less than ten minutes separate my home and the storage. I stashed there some personal artifacts I couldn't bear to leave in L.A. and preferred not to have in my apartment. A bunch of framed photos of me and my deceased parents, for example, would've meant I'm settling.

Originally, I hadn't planned on it. Hadn't intended on me and Robin happening, never thought I'd give in to temptation.

Hadn't. As in past tense.

Today, I allow myself to dream that all these things I had stashed away might find their permanent home in the Big Apple.

Because Robin isn't just Wes's daughter anymore. She's not an unattainable fantasy, either. She wants me. Practically begged me to admit our feelings are mutual when she asked why I'm taking her home with me.

And fuck, did her need to hear me say those words rattle me. My possessiveness for her is out in the open now. It urges me to claim her, have her, hug her for ages. Her plea to reciprocate her feelings for me—even in this backward manner—have changed me irrevocably.

Since that moment in the kitchen, there's no denying it anymore.

Robin is mine.

"I'm on the pill," she peeps from inside the helmet.

That sweet, little voice.

Sweet, little voice that can utter the most absolutely filthy words.

Words that had me stopping ten minutes short of my apartment. From making love to her for the first time on a clean bed or carrying her to the shower soon after.

It's too late for any of it. I can't do or concentrate on anything that doesn't involve fucking her senseless this fucking minute. Not on a damn thing.

"I wouldn't have cared if you weren't." The door slides up to the top. I drive the bike inside, pressing the remote to close the door. "Would've made no difference to me."

"You don't mean it." She sounds troubled, and maybe a little hopeful.

"Wrong." When the door rolls down, I push the bike's kickstand to the floor, turning it off. "I do. I said I'd take care of you. I said you don't have to worry."

My helmet comes off. I put it away, taking off Robin's and placing it next to mine. Her legs are open on the bike, her dress hiked up, allowing me a glimpse of her white panties.

They're a shade darker than they were this morning. They're damp, clinging to her pussy, outlining the shape of her lips. I'm going to tend to that sweet cunt, then bury myself in it here in this warehouse.

"I've wanted you long before the club." I cradle her cheeks, drawing her to me, hard.

Our lips crush into one another, our moans echoing in the enclosed space. Robin's fingers cling to my T-shirt and tug, her tongue twisting with mine. I grunt into her mouth with the fire she stokes inside me, falling deeper in love with this girl I'm not supposed to even look at the wrong way.

"Long before that." I take a breath for air, pressing my forehead to hers. "Wanted to hug you, kiss you, and fuck you for two long years, Robin."

She pulls back, her gray eyes bestial and adamant. "I want you too. I can't have you, I know I can't. But I want you."

"We'll find a solution." My hand slithers down her body as I kiss and suck on her neck. "In due time. First though, I'm making you come, baby."

"Oh—okay."

I graze my teeth along the curve of her neck up to her ear, stroke her swollen clit through her underwear. "You want your Uncle Callum to make you come, little Robi?"

She moans before saying, "Yes, please."

My shirt nearly tears under the pressure of her hold.

"Say it." My lips are at her jaw, my hand wrapping around her blond locks.

Her chest rises and falls, her mouth releasing a mixture of moan and a sharp intake of breath. "Make me come. I need it. I need you."

"That's more like it." I slide my fingers under her panties, drawing wetness from her slit and rubbing her hardened nub. "But you can do better."

I raise my head to look at her. My tug on her hair causes tears to gather at the corners of her eyes, the pleasure I'm giving her turning her gray irises to a color as black as the night.

Instead of rubbing her faster, encouraging her to come, I start tapping her clit lightly.

"I'll say anything." Her hips roll on the seat of the bike.

I pinch her clit, and thank fuck for this room being soundproof. Robin's desperate cry is mine to hear. Only ever mine.

"Greedy cunt you have." I bend to bite her bottom lip. "It'll get what it's asking for. When you say, *I want you to make me come, Uncle Callum.*"

She doesn't hesitate. "I want you to make me come, Uncle Callum."

"Fuck," I growl, turning on the ignition of the motorcycle.

The fumes don't worry me; the air ventilation system will clear them out of the unit. What I am concerned about, what's at the forefront of my mind, is giving Robin another orgasm.

"Lean on me." One of my arms wraps around her, taking her in. The other teases the hem of her panties. "Ass up."

She does as I say, and I yank her panties down to her knees. Her legs are restrained, so the pressure of thighs on her clit is added to the continuous low hum of the motorcycle's engine.

Robin gyrates on the vehicle, seeking the pleasure I promised her. I'm beyond slowing things down, well past providing her sounds other than the bikes and her rhythmic panting.

"I'm gonna make you feel good." I push down the sleeve of her oversized dress and her bra, exposing her shoulder. "Have you clenching on my fingers while you fuck my motorcycle."

"Uncle Callum."

I'm on fire when hearing the pleading edge to her voice, freeing my dick out of my boxers. I don't waste a second before kissing Robin on her pouty, gorgeous lips, twisting my tongue with hers, and guiding her palm to my lower abdomen. "Grab my cock."

Her hand is at my length, applying just the right amount of pressure, rubbing at just the right pace. Fucking perfect.

"That's it, baby." I suck on her nipple and slide two fingers between her and the seat, inside her pussy. "You stroke my cock so fucking well. Exactly how your Uncle Callum likes it."

"Thank"—she smears my precum on the head, the same thing I told her I did back in the club—"you."

My teeth close around her nipple, biting her lightly. My fingers curl inside her cunt and stroke her G spot until she squirms. Robin squeezes her thighs, her lips dropping to the top of my head.

"I'm coming." She moans into my hair. "Uncle Callum, I'm coming."

I pull away from her nipple, cupping the back of her neck and slamming her lips to mine. With her body bent forward, her clit is pressed to the heel of my palm, her pussy getting every bit of the bike's vibrations.

"Do it." I come up for air, locking our eyes together. "Let me hear you come for me."

Robin's orgasm is a magnificent display of pussy that sucks me in and sounds that reach to the darkest places in my soul. She's whimpering, cursing, begging for more all while rubbing me until I'm almost ready to burst myself.

"Come here." I gather her in my arms, lowering her to the concrete floor.

Her cheeks are ruddy, her body limp and sated.

"I'm not done with you." Standing above her, I kick off my shoes, jeans, and boxers. "Gonna fuck my dirty-mouthed girl on this dirty floor."

She eyes me hungrily as I lower to my knees, remove her panties, and spread her legs wide. Then her lips curve in a smirk.

"You like that, you filthy little thing."

"Yes."

My cock pushes against her slit. "Baby, you really are tight."

Her eyes lower to where our bodies are connected. "And you really are big."

"Still plan on fucking you hard." I press one of her thighs to the floor, pushing an inch deeper.

"Still want it."

The glimmer in her eyes is unmistakable.

So is her cry when I shove my entire length into her. I sink all the way in, not showing Robin an ounce of mercy.

"Still?" I raise an eyebrow.

"Yes, Uncle Callum." Her hands flatten on the floor. "Fuck me, take me, please."

I thrust in and out of her, watching beads of sweat form on her forehead and her ample tits bouncing the harder I fuck her. She arches her back just as I lean down to put one of them in my mouth, calling my name when I press both her knees up to either side of her belly.

The more open she is, the deeper my dick goes in her and the fiercer our connection becomes. I don't just want her. I need her. In these two weeks, our desires have dented and destroyed the heavy wall we've built between us.

We were right to do it. Back then.

A noble idea that's no longer sustainable.

I'll sort out everything to be with her. I'll find the words to get Wes to see her and I are meant for each other. It'll be okay, just as I promised her.

"Come." My cheek is on hers, her breaths caressing my neck.

Her scent is all around me—her soft perfume, shampoo, and sweat. Her body tightens on me, and I pummel into her with more force, pinning her to the ground, experiencing the rippling of her climax as it washes over her.

I release my load in her soon after, unburdening my emotions and my sperm alike.

As I caress her hair and kiss her adorable nose, I get this peaceful sense that everything's going to be alright.

It has to be.

"You're mine, Robin."

She nods and smiles, like she's known it all along.

And who knows, maybe she has.

CHAPTER FOURTEEN
Robin

Callum scoops me in his arms off the floor of the storage unit. He helps me climb onto the bike, placing the helmet on me gently. The rest of the drive to his apartment is peaceful—he offers me silence and I bathe in it, leaning into him. Loving him.

My legs are still limp, my eyes hazy when he pulls over in his building's parking lot. He doesn't need me to say it, he just knows, giving me a piggyback ride up the elevator and to his sofa.

He's done it time and again years ago.

This one, though, is a little different.

"Tea, coffee?" Callum sits next to me, running his fingers through my tangled hair. His touch and gaze send warmth and pleasant shivers all the way down to my toes.

"No, thank you." I tilt my head and melt into his palm. It's so big, like the rest of him. So comforting.

"Beer maybe?" A slow smile creeps up his lips. "You technically have one year left, to be legal, but…"

"No." My body stiffens, eyes dropping to my lap.

"Robin." He crouches lower, searching my face for answers. "What is it? You can tell me anything."

Callum's confidence is a safety net I can fall into without worrying about the outcome. I wish I could take him up on his offer. It was stupid and juvenile what I did, yet it wasn't the end of the world.

It wouldn't be for anyone else who didn't promise themselves they'd put their father first.

I can't repeat it. I won't ruin the day Callum called me his, won't taint it with a stupid story about a selfish kid.

I won't.

"I'm okay." I force my muscles to relax.

They listen, one limb at a time. I cover Callum's palm. He flips his, wrapping his fingers around my wrist and caressing it.

"I'm not in the mood for a beer. Maybe water?"

His sweet half-smile returns. "Maybe?"

"Now you're just playing with me." I let out a tired huff of a laugh.

"I'm a counselor." He moves both our palms to his lips to kiss the top of mine. "Words matter."

"I noticed." My teeth bite my bottom lip. Even through my exhaustion, the reminder of what he said to me prickles my skin in the sweetest, most decadent way. "I really like that about you, Uncle Callum."

Something sinister flashes behind his eyes. And while he doesn't act on it, I recognize it for what it is. Two years ago, I had no way of knowing.

"Uncle Call, I take your smile means you liked your Christmas presents?" I closed the French doors as I walked inside behind me.

It was a cold, snowy day in New York. The morning after Christmas. Dad installed a jacuzzi in the terrace some time before Thanksgiving, and the four of us spent our mornings, afternoons, and evenings there like we hadn't seen a jacuzzi before.

But with Callum staying at our place in his dark sweatpants and form-fitting white sweater, I didn't want to be there for long. I was hoping to talk to him.

For a few minutes, to be alone, and have all of his attention to myself.

While wearing a bathing suit and a towel wrapped around my shoulders.

His penetrating stare lingered on my body on my walk toward him, trailing up to my lips, landing on my eyes. He remained focused on me since I opened the doors until I stood right there next to him.

"Sit."

I lowered my bum to the sofa by his side, and he, as if in this silent dance where he understood me more than anyone, placed his sweater over my wet shoulders. I did my best to not sniff his cologne, as hard as it was.

"It's not the presents I'm happy about."

He scooted back a little, to my disappointment. Some days over the past couple of months, I thought he liked me. On days when he wouldn't have distanced himself from me.

"Then?" I tucked my hair behind my ear, pretending the mild rejection had done nothing to me.

"I received a call from my investigator; she says she finally got her hands on evidence to prove without a shadow of a doubt that our client isn't guilty."

Callum's piercing blue eyes leveled with me in a way that made me feel like he'd waited for me to come back inside to share this news. "I'll prove his innocence in court, and he'll walk."

My hands flew to my mouth to cover my gasp. "A Christmas miracle!"

"Yeah." The intensity of his gaze caught me off guard, his next words throwing me into a spin. "You get me, Robin."

"You're boring her with court talk again?" Mom's voice cut into our conversation.

I turned my head to her, hoping my blush didn't show. "It's never boring."

"That's all right." Callum sounded different. Not offended. Just colder.

I twisted to him. The heat I thought I saw was gone.

Then again, what the hell did I know about heated looks?

Nothing. Not back then.

The sofa dips to my right after a few moments of daydreaming. Callum's warm hand rubs my shoulders, pressing tenderly into my tense muscles.

"Here." He offers me the water glass I asked for.

His demeanor isn't the same as when we had sex, as the man he is in real life. Less demanding, softer and accepting. I don't think too many people are lucky enough to get a glimpse of that side of Callum.

Though he and his lawyer persona are very much alike—strong, fierce, and fearless—with me, on this sofa, he's different. He lets a sliver of sweetness break through the cracks.

"Thanks." Both my hands cup the glass, and I take a sip.

"How have you been? Besides your mom leaving and that asshole from work?" His brows knead together; his voice is that of penance. "I'm sorry I haven't been around to help you. So fucking sorry, Robin."

"You have nothing to be sorry for." It comes out much angrier than I intended. I lower the glass on the coffee table, the water sloshing around the glass. "There's only one person who should be sorry here, and it's Mom."

"I was in the city, goddammit." Callum leans his elbows on his thighs, dumping his head into his palms. "I live twenty minutes from you, an hour and a half from Adele. A fucking phone call away."

"Really, it's fine." My heart aches for him. We switch roles, me rubbing his muscular back. "We managed."

"It's not fine." The pain in his eyes when he finally glances up at me is palpable. "You could've told me about that asshole for the two months I've lived here. You would've known I was here to back you up no matter what. But I kept my distance. For all my talk, I'm a fucking coward."

His last sentence shakes me. To be honest, I haven't taken the time to consider why he hasn't told me he's moved. And now I feel stupid not to have brought it up earlier.

"Why didn't you tell me you moved?"

"Robin." Callum's hands encapsulate my face, his thumbs smoothing the worry lines between my eyebrows. "I couldn't be close to you without your dad present. I didn't trust myself. Because of what I feel for you. I meant what I said in the storage room; I wanted you long before today, and there's no way I could've controlled myself."

He swallows, another fracture to his impenetrable shield cracking for me. "It's wrong of me to even think about you like I have. It's wrong and I can't fucking help it."

Trepidation taints my happiness, raising my hackles. The man has been a part of my life since the day I was born, after all. It's my turn, so many years later, to scoot back from him.

"Since when did you start thinking about me…that way?"

"Fuck." He ruffles the short hair at the back of his neck, unable to meet my eyes. "I… It happened in stages, crept up on me despite my best efforts to suppress it. Somewhere after your eighteenth birthday, I started seeing you in a different light. More like a woman than a girl. You stopped being the kid who screams and laughs loudly, the sweet girl who runs everywhere around the house."

He lowers his chin, pinning his blue stare to mine. "I loved that girl to pieces, don't get me wrong. I just didn't have these kinds of feelings for her. But it was still wrong enough for me to drown out anything remotely inappropriate for months."

Air seeps back to my lungs. Eighteen is normal. It's when I began to like him differently, too. When my thoughts, other than those of having him be my first kiss, were far from innocent as well.

"I had to move out of here, couldn't see you every weekend without feeling the burn of guilt and shame. Hence, my move to Los Angeles." His fingers interlace in his lap; his thumbs thump one another in a quick *tap, tap, tap*.

Unfortunately, I'm too saddened to be turned on.

"It was my only way out of this mess."

"So, you left your life behind," I whisper, unable to talk louder. "It's my fault. I'm so sorry, Callum."

"Robin."

My breaths are short and loud. Another round of guilt overcomes me in the form of panic. I mumble, "My fault," at least a dozen times.

Callum's voice pulls me out of it.

"Robin. Listen to my voice. Breathe in. Breathe out."

Inhale, exhale.

"Look at me, please."

I muster the strength to stare up at him.

"Can I touch you?"

It's hard to believe the lengths of his selflessness. He just admitted he uprooted his life to avoid even thinking about me inappropriately. Analyzing it, I realize it's not for my sake alone, it's for Dad's, as well.

Eighteen is legal. I was over eighteen since his move to L.A., was twenty when he moved back to be next to Dad. And yet he had no intentions of meeting me alone.

And now, after everything he's done for us, he remains haunted by his conscience. Still requires my permission, in case anything he said disgusted me.

I almost cry with my love for him.

"You can."

"Thank fuck."

He pulls me in with his strong arms into his lap. I'm straddling him on either side, and his hands come up to my waist. It's innocent and intimate all at once. It's us.

"None of this is your fault." His fingers dig into my skin to show how serious he is. "No one's to blame here. That's life. Nothing to be upset over."

I scrunch my nose, refusing to let go of the guilt. Sure, I didn't do anything on purpose, but why did he have to change his life for me? I could've gone to college somewhere else. Could've done something.

Then again… Would I really, though?

Would I have told him I'm not accepting his newfound feelings, or would I have been selfish and careless to do exactly what I'm doing today?

I guess I'll never know.

"Hey, Robin, what's with the face?" His eyes dance between mine, playfulness blending into the somberness in them. "Moving to L.A. isn't the worst thing that can happen to a person."

"It's not L.A." I sigh. "It's the sacrifice."

"Giving you the time to grow up was worth it." His hands travel to my face, pulling my forehead to his. "You were worth it. You *are* worth it. And you will be worth whatever I have to do to keep you. Do you understand me?"

I did. I had my own confessions to make. They remained buried for the time being under the overload of new information that swelled my heart and shattered it to pieces.

Callum didn't ask me anything beyond that for the rest of the night. We showered, then snacked on popcorn while watching old reruns.

He cradled me under the expensive sheets of his opulent bed and, in his caring arms, I found my peace.

CHAPTER FIFTEEN
Robin

"Package for Robin Fontaine," a delivery guy calls from the reception loud enough for me to hear in my cubicle at the office.

It's been three days since Sunday. Three days since Callum drove me to my studio apartment, three days since I've seen him. I had to make up for a full no-studies Saturday and then some, and my boyfriend gave me all the space I needed to become the best version of myself.

Boyfriend.

The word curls and wraps itself around my brain, forms shapes and colors in front of my eyes. The letterings are in pink and glitter. They're laden with meaning, sinking into the depths of my heart, keeping me warm despite the physical distance.

I love him.

I really, really do.

"Robin?" Winnie waves a hand in my face. "Earth to Robin. You there?"

"Yeah." I blink a few times to rouse out of my daydreaming. "What's up?"

"Umm. Your package?" Her brows raise to add to the *duh* effect, her eyes darting to the right.

Where the delivery guy holds a box wrapped in a rich, pearl-white paper and the electronic signature tablet in the other hand.

"Oh, gosh, I'm sorry." And embarrassed. My quick stumble to my feet causes my chair to drag a little too far back.

"No worries," the guy wearing the red baseball hat says. He offers me the package, then points to the blank space where I'm supposed to sign.

"Thanks."

There's a low buzz around me. My face has to be red. I can be loud and friendly, but being the reason for my coworkers' whispers around me is too new, too awkward.

"Well?" Winnie perches her elbows on the partition. "Are you going to open it?"

I have a strong feeling of who sent it. So no, I'm not going to open it while people are watching.

Especially not after the dirty messages Callum sends me throughout the day like *The rustle of the trees reminded me of the sound of your labored breaths when I drove my fingers into your tight pussy* and *I just tapped my pen for five minutes on the desk to the rhythm I'm planning on fucking you next time we see each other.*

Or the phone sex we had this morning, when he told me to place the phone on speaker and on my pelvis. He listened to me masturbate as he tapped and clinked and said the nastiest things until we came together.

Yeah, whatever he sent me, it's not for anyone's eyes but mine.

"Are you going to give me some space?" I wink at Winnie.

She groans, slumping back to her seat. "I sure fucking hope that the bigger the secret, the bigger the dick."

My heart sinks, as warm and nurtured as it is. It hurts me to have to be Callum's secret, and have him be mine. We haven't wronged anyone by being together; we're not breaking the law. I'm not a kid anymore, and he's not in a position of power over me.

We're two people who are madly in love, have been in love for a long while. There's nothing bad about us, and yet I can't imagine a scenario of coming out with it.

I don't want our love to feel wrong, but I can't help it does.

Eva Marks

It's not the world's opinion I'm nervous about, the judgment. I don't live for them. It's for my dad. I don't want him finding out, especially not through other people.

Callum said he'll fix it somehow, so I have to accept this sinking feeling for now and hope that one day soon, he'll pull through. For us, for our family.

In the meantime, I'll have to be patient, focus on work and how to not make things weird around Winnie. I launch a crumpled paper at my teammate, laugh on cue when she does, and go to unfolding what must be a gift from him.

With my mindset shifted, a thrill of what lies inside the lightweight package runs down my spine. I peel off the paper carefully yet quickly, the battle between hating to ruin the beautiful packaging and wanting to see what's inside.

Contrary to the light wrapping, the box inside is silk black. There's no lettering on it. It looks suspiciously like Mom's fancy underwear packages she used to order a few months before she left Dad for another man.

I stumbled upon two or three of them, and she told me to keep it a secret between us. *A surprise for Dad.*

Ugh. I was so naïve.

Bile rises up my throat at the memory. It's illogical. I'm not my mother; I'm not a mistress who cheats on another man. Callum is a *single* man who sent a sexy gift to me, a *single* woman.

How many more times will I have to repeat it to myself that we're not hurting anyone? For how long?

Stop letting her actions rule your life and open it.

The lid snaps open elegantly. I sneak glances to left and right, up and behind me to make sure no one's watching, then hover over it and look inside.

The first thing I see is a handwritten note written by Callum. I'd recognize his elegant letterings everywhere.

Before I read it, all I can think about is holy shit, he went out himself and bought it for me. He could've ordered online, could've had someone write it for him, but he didn't. He made time in his insanely busy schedule with the trial coming up to go on his own and buy me a gift.

It could've been gum for all I care. The intention behind it matters. And there's so much to it.

Sigh. Be still my womb.

R,

You're in my heart 24/7. I miss you even when we talk on the phone.

I promised to give you space to study, and I will.

But after that, I'll have my lips on yours and listen to that sweet noises you make when you come all over my cock.

Wear these for me tonight, my place, 8 p.m.
Yours,
C.

My thumb strokes the note where he signed his name. My heart is a ball of light ready to explode.

Mine.

I tilt the note at an angle so a curious Winnie wouldn't be able to peek at my gift, revealing a lace set of dusty pink lingerie. The sheer bra and panties are soft, and the details on them are perfect.

Though they aren't the reason I'm instantly wet and wanting.

It's the tiny, golden bells attached to their fronts, one on each garment.

This man will be my undoing.

Butterflies and bees and angry birds swoop and swirl on the inside of my belly. If it wasn't for work, I wouldn't have waited a single minute to run to wherever he is and submit myself to whatever he has planned for us.

But I have to work. Both of us do.

Until then, I text him.

Me: *I'm yours. Not because of the gift.*

Three seconds don't pass when he answers.

Callum: *Interesting. Why, then?*

Me: *Because I never had any other choice.*
Callum: *Neither have I, Robin. Not a single one. See you at 8.*

I worked as if I were possessed today. Emails were answered within minutes, my tasks marked completed one after the other. Dallying in the office longer than necessary wasn't an option for me.

The precious lingerie set Callum sent would be wasted on me just slipping into them after a long work day. They deserved to be worn on a showered, pleasantly scented body, under clean clothes with my hair washed and dried.

I'm aware Callum doesn't care how I show up, aside from the lingerie he instructed me to put on. He's seen me in every shape and form in my twenty years of living. Dirty from running into puddles, smelly and sweaty from a volleyball game on the beach, and now added to the respectable list—being sprawled on the dirty concrete with his cum dripping from my pussy.

It's not him, it's me. I care. The set is so pretty that I want to be pretty wearing it for him.

After a scalding shower, I dry myself and put on the bra and underwear. They fit perfectly to my curves, and I'm not the tiniest bit surprised at that. Callum's hands ran across and gripped my body for hours on Saturday night. He mapped my skin, inch by inch.

He, out of everyone, should know.

I put on faded skinny jeans and a T-shirt in a lighter shade of pink. With an hour left to go, I take my time drying my hair and leave it draped across my shoulders, hoping the bike ride wouldn't mess it up too much. I apply a light coat of mascara and paint a thin strip of black eyeliner, the last items on my to-do list.

I swipe my phone off the vanity to check the time again. Seven.

Waiting for another forty minutes is parallel to a slow, painful burn. I'm going to text him and write to him to stop what he's doing and get his ass home to let me in in the next twenty minutes.

Except I don't get past typing the third word.

Three knocks on my door stop me.

Sneaky Callum. This must be a part of his plan, this added surprise. I practically run to answer him, throwing the phone on the bed that takes up half the entire apartment, and pull open the door.

"Surprise!"

My face drops all the way down to street level. I fix it as fast as humanly possible, smiling around the worry that strangles the air out of my lungs.

DAD *can't* KNOW

It isn't Dad and Adele's fault that I was about to sneak around and do what I shouldn't. Looking at him and my sister now, at the joy on their faces, the wrongness of what Callum and I are doing crushes me into a million pieces.

The two people I love the most could've caught us in the act. They would've seen through our lies and deceit. They would've felt betrayed. I know they would've.

What in the world was I thinking? Nothing Callum could do or say would make my family look at me with this pure glee ever again.

"Hey!" I hug and kiss Dad, then Adele. "Come in."

"We're actually here to take you out." Adele smiles, pinching my cheek jokingly. "I have a project at school and I won't be able to drive down here for a while. I didn't want to go over a month without you two."

Dad hugs her to his side. He looks like such a giant in my small studio. A sweet, happy giant. He scans me up and down after his examination of the apartment. "Are you about to go out somewhere? We won't be offended, we were the ones who intruded, and…"

"No, please, you never intrude."

The minute I saw them, I came to terms with rescheduling my evening with Callum. The longer I stand here and lie-slash-hide-the-truth from Dad, the more my heavy, laden heart understands this might have to be a permanent cancellation.

"Let me just text Winnie I won't join her and the rest of the team for dinner, and I'm ready to go."

"Thank you, Robi." Adele hops in place. "You won't regret it."

I stalk to the bed, swallowing back my tears and trying to forget I'm wearing the garments chosen for me.

While I could never regret family time, I can't not bring myself to be okay with letting go of the greatest love of my life.

Me: *Dad and Adele dropped by. I can't make it today. Sorry.*

I switch the phone to silent mode.

I plaster a smile on my face.

I go out with my family to a night I prayed would come for months.

Everything is as it should be yet, at the same time, none of it is.

CHAPTER SIXTEEN
Callum

I'm driving my Mercedes to my apartment on the Upper East Side of Manhattan on a cool Spring evening. I recently finished the last trial prep with my client, which went well.

Only by the grace of God and years' worth of experience.

Otherwise, I would've been consumed whole by thoughts about Robin.

Things have been going great up until yesterday. We were free around each other in person and over the phone. In love without even articulating the words. I could tell she trusted her body, her world, and future in my hands.

I had her.

Then she canceled our date. I understand why. I'm not a jerk. After the months they suffered, and given my parents were alive, most chances are I would've done the same. I don't hold any of it against her.

Truthfully, I don't blame her for anything, not her avoidance either. I can tell that sneaking around had painted her an ugly, difficult-to-digest picture. It's either lying or telling them the truth, neither of which is an easy pill to swallow.

My poor little girl. I wish I could press a button to fix it for her.

But I can't. And in the meantime, I hurt too.

I miss her. To have her taken from me is a constant punch to the gut.

As my car courses past tall buildings, designer stores, and the millionth yellow cab I see for today, I try and consider my solutions to this problem.

There are three viable ones, three stories my counselor mind can choose to tell.

One is the coward's way out—go back to Los Angeles. Wes is back to more or less his older self, calls every other day, laughs occasionally. That's what I came here for, and I couldn't be more pleased to see him gaining his life back.

My journey here is technically done. By taking a step back and disappearing, I can spare Robin weeks of madness and pain.

I would hold on to my promise and make life easier for her.

Like I mentioned, the coward's way out.

Two is an option I mulled over longer—giving her space.

The trauma of her mother leaving is fresh in her mind. Robin hasn't told me as much, but it's highly probable there's this lingering fear of how our relationship will impact the open wounds of her dad and Adele.

Taking a step back so she can process all of it might work, if that's the issue. In two, three, or ten months, life will get back on track. Her family would've healed, and I'll be here, waiting for her with open arms.

I can do that. Thing is, what will she see later when she looks at me?

My intensity, words, and promises would seem fake. It'll look like I didn't care being away, like I may have gone with someone else. I could explain myself to her, once she's ready, which she'll understand.

Though it wouldn't change how I broke my promise to be her shield. How I took the backseat, unfazed whether I had her or not.

In the long term, the pros will outweigh the cons. So, no. Not fucking happening.

Eva Marks

Which leaves me with option three. To head over to the location Garland provided me, her apartment, to make good on my promise. To stand there and tell her how I'm planning to rectify the situation.

To lay out the exact plan of how I'll hand Wes the news about us and how I'll convince him that this is the right thing for her, me, and for him as well. No one in this world would love and care for his daughter like I would. I can guarantee that.

I can fight for her, for us.

Option three it is, I decide as I round the car to Robin's street. Thank the fucking stars, someone vacates a parking space just when I drive past her apartment building.

I pull over to the curb, step outside to the street in my navy-blue suit. A young man pushes open the building's door. I hold it while checking the names on the intercom, then step inside and up to the third floor.

There's a light beneath the door that says Fontaine. I rap on it twice.

"Who's there?"

Her small voice lands inside my heart, the one that beats solely for her. "Callum."

The walls are paper thin, and I hear her footsteps approaching. There's hesitation behind the door. No questions, no movement.

She's waiting for me to be strong for the both of us.

"Let me in, Robin."

I hear her gasp at the name, followed by nothing.

"Open up, baby. I swear I'm not mad. And that I won't touch you unless you ask me to."

The door slides open an inch.

"Hey," I tell her.

"Hi." Her chin is pressed to her chest, her bare toes drawing circles on the old wooden floor.

I can demand her to look at me, if it wouldn't have felt as aggressive as touching her in this sensitive moment.

My voice is all I have. "Listen to my voice, Robin. Breathe in, breathe out."

Her chest inflates, then deflates. Her foot no longer swings around aimlessly.

Ever so slowly, her eyes lift to mine.

"Hey, Robin." My relief must be evident in my smile, but I don't care. Let her see every part of me.

"Hi, Cal." She steps back, gesturing for me to come inside. "I'm sorry."

I'm curious as to what her apartment looks like, to know more about Robin. Curiosity I'll have to satisfy another day.

She needs my full attention, and it's hers. I walk inside, leaning my back on the wall next to the door, watching her and nothing else with my hands stuck in my pockets.

"Talk to me. What's going on?"

Her gaze begins its descent to the floor.

I use my voice to stop her. "I'm not mad. I get why you canceled. I do."

"No, you don't." Robin's brows knead together. "If you would've gotten it, you wouldn't have come here."

"You're afraid of what they'll say." I level my tone, showing her the abundance of patience I have in me. That I could swim through any turbulent sea, barrel through any hurricane for her. "I promised you, I'll make your dad see reason. I won't stop until I do."

"He will never look at me the same." She hiccups. "Never."

My fists clench at my sides. My promise to her forces me to remain where I am, even though it kills me to do it.

"He will. Not too many parents love their kids like Wes loves you two." I talk to her in a voice that's equally soft and hard, not aggressive, but not yielding, either. "It'll take a hell of a lot more than dating his best friend to have him think any less of you. It'll be me he'll be upset with, not you."

"It'll be the both of us." She twists her lips to the side, pulling at the hem of her T-shirt. "Thing is, you can walk away from this. From us. I can't."

"What makes you say that?" My eyes widen to the point it hurts. "What makes you even think that? I won't leave you."

"It's not impossible. And then I'll stay with a broken heart and a father who thinks I betrayed him."

She wipes her eyes with the back of hand, destroying my heart and my resolve with it.

In two steps, one of my hands cradles the back of her head, the other is wrapped around her torso. Robin plasters her face to my chest, her silent sobs wetting my dress shirt.

Fuck my fucking shirt.

"There's a solution to all of this, baby." My hand rubs up and down her back in soothing motions. "We'll have to be patient, and it won't happen overnight. It will happen, though. And I'll stick around for every second of it and more if it means I'll end up being with you."

There's movement beneath me. I release a fraction of my hold to allow her to find my gaze. Her lips are swollen from crying; her cheeks are waterfalls of black mascara streaks.

I haven't seen such beauty in my forty-three years on this planet.

"You can't promise me you won't leave."
"The fuck I can."
"How?"

It's my turn to take a deep breath. "Because I love you, Robin. Because I've always loved you."

CHAPTER SEVENTEEN
Robin

"You can't love me," I murmur, pushing off his chest while wanting it glued to my body.

His rough gentleness encompasses me, his arms harsh barricades that won't let go. I can feel his love, can sense it in my heart.

I'm aware of how I reciprocate it with my every breath, every thought, every pulse of blood running through my veins.

Our future is laid out for me to grab with both hands.

Yet, for a staggering number of reasons, accepting it is impossible.

"Of course, I can." Callum's lips hover above mine.

Our breaths mingle, our bodies wound into an embrace I wish I never had to break.

"I love you, Robin." His nose grazes my cheek, tender and precious, and I melt for him. "I've loved you throughout your whole life. I loved you as Wes's kid, your sharp and funny attitude. Loved how you made me an uncle for the first time."

Callum pulls back, staring me dead in the eye. "You were the whole universe to your father, mother, and me. Then Adele. But you'll always be the first. And I loved you as such, as an uncle should for the longest time. My love was pure and honest."

His genuine speech overwhelms me. It swallows up the space of the room, and with it, every living cell in my lonely heart. Callum isn't a predator. He hasn't been grooming me. The truth in his words is carved into his skin. I believe him.

I understand him, too.

I loved him the same way a child would love her uncle. Until I didn't.

"Then,"—he continues—"you changed. You grew in front of me. You became a young woman."

His lips twist in an apology. I wish to wipe it off his handsome face. He shouldn't apologize for what I'm just as guilty of feeling for him. But my tongue is heavy in my mouth, and sewing words into a neat sentence isn't something I'm capable of.

"You're the same person, only slightly modified." Through his gaze and the gentle swipe of his thumbs on my lips, I sense him heating up. Yet he controls it, bottling it behind a mask of his stoic expression. "And so is my love."

I have the urge to grab his lips, to feel the words as he says them. In a way, they're not real. I've longed to hear them for two years, so that it seems like a wicked trick of the mind. But then he continues to talk, and I continue to eat them up.

"I love how your laugh grew huskier, how you're able to hold down an adult conversation with me. I love it when you sit next to me when I tell you to breathe as I order." His lips twitch at the satisfaction the memory evokes. "You fill a hole in my life I never knew was that fucking empty. I couldn't *not* love you."

"Callum…" is what my feeble mouth allows me to say as I sway toward him.

"Baby, I need to finish this." He kisses my nose. It's a sweet gesture, belying his need in the form of his hardening cock. "I fell for your body like I fell for your personality. Your pouty lips." He pinches my bottom one between his fingers, then bites it.

"Your curves." His hand runs from my back to my collarbone, flattening against it.

Callum doesn't leave it there. He traces it down to the front of my breasts, the side of my body, cupping my ass. Callum's fingers slide up, digging into my waist.

I'm wet and feeble, putty in his big, dominant hands. He presses me to his front forcefully, to his thick, hard cock and huge, soft heart.

"You were barely a couple of months older than eighteen, and I hated myself for wanting you. Fucking despised myself for it, two years later. That's why I went away, Robin. That's why I haven't reached out."

It was hard to fathom this piece of information the first time I heard it. Doesn't get any easier in the second round.

"I couldn't hurt you or Wes, even if my fantasies were limited to my imagination." His mouth pinches into a tight scowl. "And last thing. You must know, moving to the other side of the country didn't make me love you any less. What I feel for you, this isn't some oversimplified emotion like affection or caring. It really is love. All-consuming, ever-lasting love."

I whimper-sigh, and he captures my dire breath with his lips. He destroys me with his kiss while thrusting a new passion for life into me. His tongue dives past my teeth, his growl rattling my bones.

He's right.

It really is love.

Not for me, though. For this perfect woman he pictures me to be.

DAD *can't* KNOW

I have to tell him how selfish I am. How I'm not what he thinks.

Soon.

I'm yearning for a little more of his pure, unadulterated love. To be his sweet, immaculate Robin for another minute or two.

Fuck, I'm so desperate at this point that I'll take another second.

My body, torn and wrecked by my emotions, betrays me. Two tears of desperation and craving for him roll down my cheeks, landing on where Callum's and my lips connect.

His eyes flutter open, studying mine. The thumbs I love so much banish tear after tear.

"Did I scare you off?"

"No." I draw in a shaky breath, gathering my courage. "It's just you can't love me. Not the real me."

"I disagree. I'll love you in any shape, however you come to me, Robin Fontaine." He kisses my nose, adding, "Talk to me. Please."

"You see me as this amazing, put-together person. It's a lie. I'm not her." My voice slips. I swallow my stupid sob and shame, knowing this has to be said. "The day Mom left, I vowed I'd look after Dad. Adele did her best to visit and call whenever she could, but I'm the one who lives next to him. He's been the best dad for twenty years, and I owed it to him to be the best daughter when he had no one else, to repay him an ounce of the love he's given me."

"You are, Robin. He knows you are."

My eyes bounce around the room. Anywhere except to the man who thinks so highly of me, when I clearly don't deserve it.

"One month." I huff out a laugh without an ounce of mirth to it. "Couldn't be that person for one fucking month."

The fact Callum says nothing makes it easy to talk to him. Heartbreaking, too, to be reminded of that day.

"Dad and I were watching a movie; I don't even remember which one. It threw him back to his and Mom's first date. That's all I can remember, because that's what he mumbled before clamping up."

I'm gutted from the flashbacks of that night. Despite my clogged throat and pained heart, I keep on talking, "I looked at him when he hadn't said anything for a few minutes after that. He was crying *again*, Callum. My father cried big, silent tears like he didn't want to be a bother or anything. He was feeling miserable, and I was the one who lost it. I waited for him to fall asleep, draped a blanket over him, and went out to drink."

DAD *can't* KNOW

"Robin, baby." Deep, blue eyes pierce into my soul. "You can't blame yourself for wanting to forget."

"I—"

Callum places his arm beneath my butt, hiking my feet up in the air. My legs wrap around his waist. I allow him to carry me to my bed where he sits the both of us down with me straddling him. He's no longer hard. He's enveloping, cherishing.

And I don't fucking deserve it.

"You're entitled to break down. To look for escapism." He brushes a damp strand of hair behind my ear, his fingers lingering on my cheeks.

"It's much worse than escapism." I pinch my eyes shut. "Jenna took me out to a bar, and I ordered a bottle of vodka. I had one shot after the other. She told me to stop, and I didn't. She took the bottle, and I stole it back, gulping it down clean. I drank more than half of it before I started throwing up and then I… I…"

My face crumples when I break down in the mother of all ugly cries. Callum's palm cradles my nape, drawing me to his chest. I don't ever want to leave here.

"I fainted. The bar owner called an ambulance. Jenna called Dad." I tilt my head to Callum's warmth, the shame becoming too big for me to contain by myself. "He was worried and scared and yet he kept hugging me and telling me how much he loves me. I added to his pain, and he still found it in himself to love me."

"Wes will never not love you, Robin."

I lift myself up to face Callum. This next part is gonna hurt like a bitch, yet it has to be said. Face-to-face.

"He won't, but I can't go through another round of embarrassing him or hurting him. He's been through enough, Callum." I let it sink in, witnessing his brow wrinkle with apprehension. "He'll love me through this. He'll love you through this. That's just the man he is. A rough Wall Street man by morning, a gentle human being by night. I can't abuse his kindness."

"I swear to you." Callum flips me on my back, his strong forearms bracketing me.

Being turned on by his strength and the vehemence in his posture is immoral. I should stop this. I should focus on what I planned on telling him. That I can't be feeling this, that there can be no us.

"Callum…"

"Quiet. I will be responsible to my friend's heart and yours," he continues. "My soul belongs to you. You see it, and he'll see it. I'll explain it to him, tell him my intentions are pure. That you and I are forever. No other man will know you like I do, no one will love you as profoundly as I do. I'll make sure that for the rest of your life you'll give me that beautiful smile at least once a day, and in return you'll always be reminded of how loved and adored you are. That's what life with me will be like. And I can't imagine anyone not wanting that for their daughter."

His penetrating glare leaves me. In its place, Callum's lips skim across my cheek, down the line of my jaw. He sucks on my neck just as he pulls my leg behind his back, plastering my body to his.

Callum is everywhere. He's my everything.

His closeness releases the heavy weight off my chest. Then, finally, words—meaningful fucking words—explode out of me. "I love you, Callum."

His face whips up, his nostrils flaring. "Again."

My chest heaves and I can barely speak. "I… I lo—"

"Be my little brave girl, Robin. Say it."

"I love you."

"That's it." His hand slithers between us, flicking open my jeans button and lowering my fly. "I love you back." He shoves his hand under my panties, looking at me while thrusting his middle finger inside my slit.

"Love that wet, dripping pussy." His lips assault mine, coaxing them open. He groans into my mouth, adding, "Wanna fuck it raw, tear you up then build you back up again. Tell me you want it."

Eva Marks

Callum is a force, a God, the oxygen I breathe. Being together with him will be a struggle; it'll be painful and it'll hurt my dad. I'm cognizant this isn't going to be easy.

But can I really live without Callum? Can I lie to myself and claim to have zero issues seeing him at family functions and talk to him like before, or worse, accept that one day he'll date someone else? Marry her?

The answer is simple. No, I can't.

He and I will have to plan this through, have a sit down with Dad. Explain it as Callum envisioned it. In a responsible, mature way, so he'll understand.

It's our only choice.

"I do." I place my hands on his face, calling for his attention. "We can't do it here, though. After last night, Dad might show up again and I have nowhere to hide you."

"You're right. Except…" He lowers himself to the waistband of my jeans, pulling them down.

"What are you doing?"

His dark eyes glimmer. "I remember sending you a gift yesterday. We're not going anywhere until you have it on you."

CHAPTER EIGHTEEN

Callum

I should tell her *Welcome to your new home.* Offer her something to drink.

But I'm a selfish bastard, so I don't.

We talked enough on the drive over to my apartment. Well, I did, mostly. I told her I'm moving to the city for her, that Edwin won't mind. I told her all the ways I'm going to make it work, though I doubt she heard any of it.

She was too busy fisting my cock above my pants and kissing my neck in my car for a long, agonizing twenty minutes.

So no, I'm not offering her a drink or a warm welcome. I'm offering my baby a rough fuck that'll leave her bruised and marked for days.

From my place on the sofa, my eyes skim over her long legs in her tight jeans. They roam up to her black T-shirt, landing on her hungry eyes. She stands with her back to the window; the red-and-purple setting sun is the perfect backdrop to my perfectly imperfect girl.

"Take your sneakers and socks off." My voice is rugged, the lust clutching at my vocal cords.

Robin kicks them off to the side, taking a step toward me. In her gaze is a silent question. *What's next?*

I push my coffee table to the side, get up and walk around her as I consider what to do next. There's a heavy armchair next to the long sofa. I lift it up and place it in front of me.

"Come over here." With a gesture of my chin, I indicate the space between me and the armchair. "Stay standing."

The question in Robin's expression doesn't stop her from sidestepping the chair. Less than a foot separates my parted knees and Robin when she does.

"Strip for me. Leave nothing on but your bra and underwear."

Her shirt goes first, jeans after. She's beautiful, more than I could've ever imagined the day I bought this for her. Her bare pussy shows through the sheer fabric, the nubs of her pink nipples are stretched for me, poking at the thin garment.

Every curve and every inch of her body are gorgeous. And this woman belongs to me.

"Very good." I grip either side of her waist and drag her to me. "My beautiful, good girl."

My mouth goes to her center, my lips wrapping around her clit. Her juices destroyed the panties, and I don't give a fuck. She tastes like fucking heaven.

Her hands grab my head, fingers digging into the roots of my hair. I suck on her clit, my tongue lapping along the fabric to the sound of her moans echoing in the apartment.

I slip two fingers under the lace, stroking her wet slit and looking up at her. "That dripping pussy wants my cock bad, doesn't it?"

"M-hmm." She nods, so weak she is barely able to hold herself up.

Standing up, I spin to stand behind Robin. One arm wraps around her midriff to hold her steady and stroke her pussy while I tilt her body forward. I place her hands on the back of the chair, leaning my weight on her to have her upper body parallel to the floor.

"What a spoiled little pussy you got." I slide my hand out of her underwear, slapping her clit hard.

Robin jostles. The bell attached to her panties jingles, the sound coming out of her throat vacillating between a moan and a cry. I get off on that sound coming out of her, spanking her pussy a second time.

"It's gotten used to my sounds, to how I create ASMR symphonies for it until you come. Am I right?"

I slam my hand on her pussy, cupping it and rubbing it over her panties with my middle finger. She cries my name, her head falling forward.

My lips brush over her hair as I plaster my chest to her back, whispering, "Answer me, Robin."

"Yes," she mumbles. "Fuck, yes. Whatever you say."

"I don't think you're really getting it." I pull back, observing her.

Robin's knuckles are white from the pressure of digging them into the chair, and her bare back is round like that of a purring cat.

Oh, she's definitely going to purr for me today.

She spins her head to me after I spend long minutes watching her in silence. Her right cheek is flushed, and her wanting face is a sight of pure seduction.

I tap my finger on my chin, now that I have her attention. Her desire. Her willingness to play along and be completely at my mercy as well as my protection.

"How are we going to make you understand what it is I want?"

"Uncle Callum," she whines. "Please."

"No begging." I take a seat on the sofa. My fingers wrap around her thighs, dragging her closer.

"What's going to happen here,"—I peel her panties off to the sound of the clinking bell—"is *you'll* be the one making sounds for *me*."

"Yes."

"You'll also be doing most of the work today until I decide to fuck you." I draw her wetness to her clit, twisting the swollen nub between my fingers. "Do we have an understanding?"

"Yes, Uncle Callum." She opens her legs, putting her pink cunt and tight pucker on display for me.

"Such a good girl."

Her legs don't quiver, moving dutifully when I tug them to me one last time. I place two hands on each of her butt cheeks, pressing them up before I dip my tongue inside her slit. I tongue fuck her for a few seconds, then pull back.

"No!"

"Quiet." My voice is thunderous, to match my slap on her ass.

A clear drop of arousal slides down her thigh. It's a torment, to witness her dire state of need and not fuck every hole in her body. But what I'm about to do will make fucking her eventually that much more worth it.

"What I'll need you to do, if you want my tongue anywhere near that desperate pussy, is fuck my mouth."

Her head twists to look at me. "H-how?"

I tilt my head to the side, meeting her gaze. "What does it sound like, Robin?"

"I don't—"

Moving back, I curl my fingers around the fronts of her thighs, slamming her cunt to my lips. My nose is at her ass, her juices dripping down my stubble. There's nothing graceful about this.

Then again, I didn't choose a fully submissive woman. I fell for Robin's strength as well as her complete admiration. I love her for her quick comebacks, for how she matches my attitude. That's my woman, and I'm going after everything she has to offer.

"Does the example satisfy the lady?"

She grunts. "In more ways than one."

"There's the mouth I was looking for." I chuckle, dark and filled with all the love I have for her. "Fuck my mouth, Robin. Fuck it hard, make a symphony with that bell attached to your bra."

My hand smacks her round, soft ass like an exclamation mark. "And don't you dare stop until you come so hard, I won't be able to hear the bells over your screams."

Her knees and elbows bend, her ass raising higher.

"I'm right here, baby." I place my hands on it, gentler this time. "Fuck. My. Face."

Her blond hair bobs when she nods. Then her pussy starts ramming into my mouth. My hands aren't applying any pressure on her; they're not guiding her pace. They're just there to direct her sweet holes to my lips.

Robin does the work I instructed her to, thrusting her dripping cunt to my face.

My mouth sucks on her for a brief second, my tongue lapping her wet hole, then the other, and all the while the bells ring and chime around us. I need her to feel more, am keen for her orgasm to be a violent wave of pleasure.

"Slow down." I stand above her, waiting until she does. I can see her ass clenching, aching. She mesmerizes me with how well she switches to her obedient side. Fucking incredible.

"We established you trust me, right?"

"I do."

"Have you ever had anything in your ass before?"

Her thighs squeeze harder. I can already feel how tight she's gonna be when the day comes that I take her from behind.

"I guess I have my answer," I smirk, gathering saliva in my mouth and parting her buttocks wide. "I won't be fucking your virgin ass today, but I am going to open you up. And we'll start with this."

I spit on her lower back, sitting while it drips down her pucker. She shudders as the fluid dampens the sensitive bundle of nerves, moaning to my thumb probing her pussy for more of her juices.

She clamps on my thumb protruding her ass, her breath leaving her in a loud huff.

"Robin, baby." I massage circles on the rim of her pucker. "Listen to my voice."

"Yes." Her voice is tight, breathless.

"Relax your ass for me. I have you."

As if pressing a button, she softens with a long sigh.

"Good girl." My thumb goes into her ass, my spit and her juices easing my entrance. Lowering myself back to my seat and my lips back to her entrance, I repeat my command, "Make that bell ring, sweet Robin."

Her compliance is immediate. She grinds herself on my face, taking it up her ass with abandon. I open her up with one hand, my tongue and teeth pleasuring her clit while my thumb sinks deeper to the last knuckle.

She's close. Her thrusts are more erratic, and the fucking bell chimes are the equivalent of a fire alarm.

Despite what I said about making her work for it, I can't stay idle. I pull out my thumb, flick my tongue on the rim of her pucker, and pump three fingers in her pussy.

The screams and convulsions I've been waiting for follow fast behind. I'm quick to dispose of my shoes and clothes as she shakes and cries, hanging for dear life on the chair. In less than a minute I'm fully naked, ready to prolong Robin's orgasm with my cock inside her.

Again, with my ass on the sofa, I hold onto Robin's waist. I twist her to face me, shifting her shivering body to position her on top of me.

She's aligned just where I want her.

To land right on my cock when I raise my hips to thrust deep into her.

"Oh." Her head bows down.

"You know who I belong to?" I sink my fingers to her thighs, moving her to pound my dick. Gripping her hand, I place it on my heart. "Who owns *this*?"

Gray eyes glance up, seeking mine. She smiles seductively. "Me?"

"Yeah, you do." I return my hand to her thigh, increasing the pace. "And who makes my cock so hard I can hardly think straight?"

She answers between moans, "I do."

"That's very true. Now ride it, Robin."

Bare of any inhibition, my beautiful blond nymph starts rocking herself on me. Her fingernails scratch at the small hairs of the bottom of my stomach, her bells ringing in tune with each sway of her hips.

Slipping a hand behind her back, I snap open her bra and toss it somewhere. It's her tits I want to see, her voice I want to hear.

"Who are you fucking?" The words come out of ground teeth.

"You." She doesn't pause, taking my entire length again and again. "Only you."

"That's a given. You're mine." I slap her breast. "Say my name."

"Callum." Her clit rubs on my skin, her breasts bouncing to her rhythm.

I slap her other breast, then grab her chin. "Uncle Callum. Say it."

"Oh, my God, yes." Robin wretches out of my hold, gripping my stomach harder. Her eyes ensnare mine, young and happy and a million shades of dark. "I love riding you, Uncle Callum."

My palm connects with her ass. "Louder."

"You make me feel so fucking good, Uncle Callum."

"Good girl." I find her clit, rubbing it the way she likes it.

"Uncle Callum," she pants. "I'm a—I'm about to come."

"Do it," I growl, feeling my own orgasm taking over me. "Come, little Robin, come on my cock."

"Uncle Callum!" she yells, spasming on me just as I come inside her.

Just as the door opens behind Robin's back.

"What the fuck do you think you're doing to my daughter?"

CHAPTER NINETEEN
Callum

Robin is frozen in place. On my dick. With her dad, who also happens to be my best friend, standing there.

She doesn't move, her eyes horrified and unfocused. She's checked out, a luxury we can't afford. Each millisecond that courses between the three of us is an eternity. Especially for my best friend who should've never, ever been subjected to this.

I'm fast to pull her up and place a throw blanket from the sofa to cover her limp and unresponsive body. I ache for the lack of ability to comfort her. I also shouldn't let the situation escalate.

I keep quiet and dress up.

By the time I have my boxer briefs on and turn around, Wes is in my face.

Him, and his fist.

It connects to my jaw, thrusting my head to the side.

I do nothing to reciprocate. I have this coming for not being as careful as I promised her.

"Out of the entire female population in New York."

Both of his hands push at my chest. Wes and I are about the same height and size, have a similar working-out regime. I stumble back half a step, not raising my hands to defend myself. I earned it.

He shoves me again. "Out of every fucking woman in L.A."

His palm is at my throat, and I say nothing. He's earned the right to let out the anger of my betrayal. "Out of all the women in the entire fucking world, you had to go for *my* daughter? *My* Robin?"

I swallow, sucking in shallow breaths.

"Answer me!" My best friend's eyes are red with rage.

We're eye-to-eye, almost nose-to-nose. I've witnessed, interrogated, and cross-examined hundreds of people over the years. I can read their expressions, can tell you exactly what will come out of their mouths next.

And as of this minute, Wes isn't ready for my apology. He isn't ready for an explanation, not even close to being ready to hear me say *I love your daughter.*

He draws his free hand back, and I ready myself for another blow.

"Dad, don't!"

"Robin, get dressed and go wait for me in the car." His gray gaze, so much like his daughter's, locks on to mine.

"No. I'm not moving." From behind Wes, I watch her scramble for her clothes, pulling them on as she speaks.

Wes grabs me by the shoulders and shakes me, seething. "Stop looking at her."

"Dad, it's not his fault." She doesn't sound like she's moving anymore, her voice steady.

"Robin, to the car. Now. I'm not asking you a third time."

Slender, dainty fingers appear at Wes's shoulder. "It's my fault, too."

At that, Wes releases me and whips back to her. My throat hurts. My heart hurts tenfold. Being with her is the best thing that ever happened to me. We're two consenting adults. This shouldn't feel this way, like we're to blame.

"Sweetheart, none of this is your fault." Her father doesn't hesitate a second before hugging her.

I take this reprieve to put my pants on. This isn't a situation to be handled in your underwear.

"You're young and kind and impressionable. He conned you into this. But don't worry." Wes's back tenses, his voice a low growl. "I'll make him pay."

"No." She wrestles out of his hold. "If this hurts you…"

Robin hides her face in her palms. Her shoulders quiver as she takes a step back toward the door. "If this hurts you, Dad, I'm sorry. I'll put an end to it."

Jesus, what a fucking torment to stay still and be this useless piece of shit when she's crying like this.

"I won't apologize for it, though." She removes her hands from her face, exposing tear-stricken cheeks and bloodshot eyes. "I love him. I've loved him like this for over two years. Before he even said anything."

My heart mends faster than it was ruptured. She has the power to heal me in a single sentence. When it was just the two of us, I did most of the declarations. I didn't mind being the side who loved the other more.

Love isn't about what I can take from the other person; love is about what I can give them.

"He should've *never* so much as thought about you that way." Wes turns his head to me, taking a step in my direction again. "You fucking predator. I let you into my house, around my family, for what? So you could groom my daughter? Influence her to fall for you?"

"Dad! Please! It's not like that."

"Robin, you should really go to the car." I hold very still, not leaving Wes's glare. "This is between your dad and me."

"No!" Her scream pounds against the cage of my heart.

Even though I wish the circumstances could've been different, I can't deny how proud I am of her. She's become a woman in her own right, a person who could conquer the world.

But still. As strong as she is, I promised her I'll never leave her stranded.

Never let her go.

"Robin," I call her without leaving her dad's eyes. "Come here."

My arm opens, sensing her drawing near me.

"Robin." Wes's wounded expression doesn't deter me. Nothing ever will, where Robin is concerned.

I glance down at her, watching her whisper, "I love him."

"And I love her." My words are sharp. There's no mistaking my sincerity. "I love her. I'll be the best partner for her, best husband, best father for our children. I've only loved her a few months short of her eighteenth birthday, and I can't stop. I'll fucking love her to the day I die."

"The age doesn't matter," Wes seethes. "This should never have happened. Ever."

"*Shouldn't* isn't a factor in our equation anymore." I squeeze Robin tighter to me. "You'll have to accept it. Deep down, you know it's what's best for her. No other man, and I mean No. Other. Man. will ever love her like I do."

"And I'll never love anyone like I love Callum."

Wes turns from us. For the long moments he paces back and forth in my living room, I'm worried he'll break Robin by walking off.

"I've always hoped you and your sister would find a partner *like* my best friend." He huffs a shaky laugh, threading a hand through his hair. "Be careful what you wish for, right?"

His gaze shifts to me, then to Robin.

He sighs a long, exasperated sigh. "Is this what you want, Robin? You're sure it's all you?"

"Yes, Dad."

"You have my blessing, then. If you're happy, I'm happy." He points a finger at me, his gaze clouding. "One tear from her and they'll find your body under the Brooklyn Bridge. Friend or no friend."

Yeah, we're gonna have to work on that.

"I would never."

I don't move toward Robin until Wes is out the door.

Eva Marks

Alone, just her and me, I'm taking my woman.

My hands swarm her body, my lips suck and kiss hers and every exposed piece of her skin. Then, and until long after the sun rises in the sky, her and I create every imaginable sound.

The sounds of our love.

EPILOGUE
Robin

One year later

Breathe in, breathe out.

I try. I really do.

It's just hard that what little air flows into my lungs rises up in a gag.

Not again.

"Robi?" Callum's deep voice reaches me from outside his bathroom.

Our bathroom.

We've been together for a year now, and I still sometimes call this his place. Not for long, though. Soon, we'll be moving out of his rented apartment into a penthouse we chose together. In the adjacent building.

Eva Marks

It sounds silly, but for us, it's what made all the difference. We chose it as a couple, we'll decorate it as a couple, and we'll live in it as a *couple.*

Our history is incredible; the friendship we've built for years, the mutual respect and private jokes, the platonic affection and care. We wouldn't have had the connection we share today without it.

I'm incredibly grateful for what we were. I'm more than grateful for this fresh start.

Sure, there's the odd stare here and there whenever we go to an event that my father's friends, acquaintances, or business partners attend. There are paparazzi photos, too, though thankfully they are rare.

And however upsetting these whispers and articles should be, they don't bother me one tiny bit. Callum proves to me every day anew how true he is to his word. He stands up to anyone who dares say something about me or looks at me the wrong way, and has already filed a few libel suits to make a few newspapers apologize to us.

I'm not surprised they hinted at this shit about me being groomed by Callum, and yet I won't stand for that lie. Not me and not Dad or Adele. On the rare occasions they get asked about it, my family will always answer what's on their hearts—they love me, they love Callum, and they couldn't have been happier for us.

Life's a peach.

Oh, no, I can't think about peaches. I can't, I can't, I can't…

I grab the sides of the toilet and vomit what's left of my breakfast.

"I'm okay." I wipe my mouth with the back of my long shirt, resigned to the fact I'll have to change it before work. "Really, don't wait for me. I'll take the bike to work."

The bathroom's floor is chilly beneath my fingers. It would be so nice to rest my pounding head on it.

Slowly, I lower to the marble white floor, close my eyes, and hug it.

Gah, that's nice.

The air shifts in the bathroom, suddenly colder and denser all at once.

"Baby." Soles of expensive shoes somewhere around me.

My head is being raised in a tender gesture, then placed on a charcoal-gray fabric. The hair that stuck to my face is being tucked away by rough and gentle fingers, the same ones that grip my chin and twist me to meet the most beautiful set of blue eyes I've ever seen.

"Hey," I whisper, my lips curving up at the sight of him. "I said I'm okay."

"Like hell." Callum rests the back of his palm on my forehead. "No fever. That's good."

"I told you." My head is heavy, sinking a little more into Callum's thigh. "I'm probably developing lactose intolerance. My stomach can't stand it."

His brow furrows deep in thought. "You haven't had anything with lactose the past twenty-four hours."

"Then gluten." The soft light of the vanity lights gives me a headache. I roll to his stomach to hide beneath the lapels of his jacket. "Must be it. Go to the office. I threw up most of it. I'll be fine."

"Not going anywhere with you like this." Callum peels his jacket off my face, just enough to look into my eyes. "When was your last period?"

Doing any sort of summing and detracting contributes to my headache. I guess the most plausible answer. "Last month."

"You sure?"

I close my eyes, get dizzy, open them. "Yes, I'm sure. Last month, in April."

He strokes my back, running his hand up and down along my spine. My purr is accompanied by his soft chuckle, and my eyes drift shut.

"Robin, my love, today is June fifteenth." His voice sneaks into my sleep, robbing it from me in a flash.

"What?" I snap up. The world spins around me, only settled by Callum's palms cradling my face. "How?"

"You studied hard, and worked. And then there was house hunting." He kisses my nose. "The days slipped by. It happens."

"But… but… we were careful." I force myself to remember what happened the past three months because, at this point, I have no other choice. "Oh, fuck. It was two days, Callum. I missed two days of pills."

"Would you be sad about it?"

I gasp and get another round of nausea for it. Callum holds my arms, and I speak between coughing. "I…would…never."

"Shh. Don't talk."

He helps me up to the vanity, dampening a washcloth and patting it along my face. In his strong arms, he carries me to our bed.

"Would you?" I ask.

"Fuck, no." Callum's lips brush mine. "I'll be the luckiest man in the world to have a baby with you."

"Good," I say in a croaked voice. "I would also be the luckiest woman alive to have a baby with you."

School can wait; work can wait. If I'm pregnant with the man I love so dearly, I'm having it.

His smile is warmer than the sun and more powerful than thunder. It's even more glorious when he returns fifteen minutes later, carrying ten different pregnancy tests.

And it's unequivocally effervescent as, one by one, they all turn out positive.

I'm choked by tears, joy, and life. On the marble floor again, with his back to the wall and my back to his chest, I feel like I won the mother of all lotteries.

I won life.

The End.

DAD *can't* KNOW

Eva Marks

About the Author
Writing edgy spicy novellas, addicted to HEAs, and an avid plant lady.

Stay in Touch!
Newsletter for new releases:
https://bit.ly/3c3K2nt
Instagram: https://bit.ly/3QQ3Nh4
TikTok: www.tiktok.com/@evamarkswrites
Facebook Group, Eva's Readers:
https://bit.ly/3LnFpln
Website: https://www.evamarkswrites.com

More Books from Eva Marks

Blue Series
Little Beginning, book #0.5
Little Blue, book #1
Little Halloween, book #2
Little Valentine, book #3

Adult Games Series
Toy Shop, book #1
A New Year's Toy, book #2

Standalones
Primal
Dad Can't Know
I'll Be Watching You — Coming August 1, 2023

Eva Marks

I'll Be Watching You
Coming August 2023—continue reading for the prologue

She doesn't know it yet, but I'll be watching. And she *will* be mine...

I'm a scientist. I work in a pharmaceutical company, finding cures and helping others.
At least that's what I do in the daytime...
At nights, in the darkness of my home, I'm a voyeur.
But I don't just watch *anyone*. I watch *her*. Just *her*.
Sloane is my complete opposite. She doesn't do *anything* in the shadows. She's an exhibitionist—a performer. I've been stalking her podcast for two years.
I'm also her new neighbor…with a view into her apartment.
Being so close and not being able to touch her is torture. I want her so much it hurts.
I *need* her.
And I'm *done* with just watching.

I'm coming for you, Sloane. Ready or not…

Pre-Order on Amazon now

DAD *can't* KNOW

I'll Be Watching You—Coming August 1, 2023

PROLOGUE

Emmanuel

Manhattan's fall holds its own kind of dark magic.

Masses of leaves in red and orange hues paint the town in all shades of earth-tone colors. They appear on the trees first, the branches billowing in the early winds of the season resembling a fire coursing through the streets, predicting the chaos of the nearing winter.

When they fall on the sidewalk, before being cleared out, their semblance of blood drops on the gray stones reminds me of something sinister.

And in this clandestine atmosphere, that's where I thrive.

That's why I've grown to love this season above all else during the ten years I've been a New Yorker, and I've observed the four of them closely.

Just as I take note of the boutique stores, bars, and restaurants decorating the street of my new apartment in SoHo on my way home from work. Of the tourists speaking in varying languages, neighbors contemplating the meaning behind their existence, their art, the climate.

I see it all. I never engage.

Because that's what I do.

I watch.

As a scientist for the past two decades, I've been studying the findings my lab experiments produce since I was a sixteen-year-old in high school. My profession imprinted in me those learning patterns, where opening my eyes to wonder about my surroundings and analyzing them has become second nature.

But my driven need to look isn't limited to inanimate objects or any random passerby.

No. It reaches far past that. It's the vice I live with, the burden I carry, the secret I mask behind a successful career and a somber expression.

I'm a voyeur.

And it's that kind of sickness that I plan on feeding tonight.

The renovated elevator takes me up to the top floor, the third where I live. I don't bother switching the lights on when the doors open to the dark hallway.

Though I have to reach the end of the narrow passageway to my apartment door, I prefer walking in the shadows. Better than being the object a nosy neighbor might glare at through their peephole.

It's not like I'm paranoid. But if anyone's going to be doing the looking, it's me.

My keys to the lab, my apartment building, and my home clink on the keychain when I fish them out of my shoulder bag where I keep my laptop.

Both travel with me wherever I go, always, unless it's a short trip downstairs, which is why I have a safe installed at home. They hold my secrets guarded against the outside world, the ones of GeneOrg, my workplace, along with the personal ones that'd get me fired and cast out of society as if I were a criminal.

I've gone to lengths to ensure I wouldn't be. I've been aware of tendencies ever since the urge to see overtook me like a storm as a teenager, and I have been trying to blend into society without letting my sickness bleed out of its confinements.

I've done everything in my power to respect women's privacy, to only peep at women who consent to it. Thanks to the internet and the wonderful free market concept of supply and demand, I lurk on the willing ones.

Women who record podcasts or videos or live streams of them prancing around their homes or having sex or reenacting this scene or the other.

Or better yet, for the past two years, *one*.

I open the door to my small kingdom, the haven I escape to where I can act on my deepest, darkest desires. The modern table lamp I have on the console where I dump my keys emanates a soft, low glow.

It doesn't light up the open kitchen and the living room, but it's enough for me to navigate to the table below the window.

My private, obscure corner behind rolled-down blinds.

No one would point a finger at me here, call me a freak, a thirty-six-year-old successful man who's incapable of asking a woman out.

The ruler of my kingdom, preparing to meet my woman.

Sitting down in the chair at the window, I fire up my laptop. A Band-Aid, whiskey, and a clean tumbler are already set neatly on my desk. I arranged them the way I liked it this morning so my flow isn't interrupted, so I can just act on my desires without overthinking what I'm doing and just proceed to follow the steps I repeat every time.

First, I attend to the webcam of my laptop, sealing both it and the secret aspect of my life. The blue of my eyes in my moments of weakness and perversion is mine alone.

Second, I pour myself three fingers of the drink to give me the final push, to relieve me from the constraints of the inhibitions I know I should possess.

The amber liquid sloshes around in my glass as I swirl it around. Using my other hand, I click on the link to her website.

Seraphine Mallory.

My dick grows painfully hard imagining the cadence of her voice even before I press play, tempting yet unassuming. Vibrant and desirable while managing to still sound attainable, within reach for her pack of voyeurs.

Knowing others jerk off to her doesn't bother me, doesn't make me think less of her. It's her job, her talent. On the contrary, my admiration for her is endless for putting herself out there. She's never shown her face, but she reveals plenty, more than I, a person in the shadows, could ever dream of.

And with that final thought, I pull up the episode I've been craving today, letting her voice fill the void in my apartment.

"The nights have been colder, the subtle hints of winter becoming more prominent. October flew by too fast. Did you feel it, too?"

To her sensual sigh, I gulp the last of my drink.

"However, my fridge doesn't care about the weather outside. So, on this cold November day, I had to jog from the grocery store. Two minutes inside the store was all it took for the sky to break and that's when I heard those little drops of rain pelting against the store's awning."

I open the fly of my sage-green slacks, relaxing in my chair as I free my thick erection from my boxer briefs.

"See, despite the cold, the sun was out when I went outside, but the bad, bad weather tricked me. I looked outside, horrified, then back at my white T-shirt, realizing it wouldn't survive the trip home..."

My eyes close, picturing this little woman stressed out about her shirt about to be drenched soon, wondering if she had a bra on. In the slow rubs of my cock, I see myself beside her on the dairy aisle, noticing her distress, considering whether I should offer her my help.

I want to. Fuck, do I need to come harder, knowing I could look. That I could've maybe approached her...

"It left me no choice but to make a run for it once the cashier rang up my milk."

I groan, feeling my balls tighten and my dick swell. Every time I hear her say *milk* I lose myself a little more, aching for her pussy to squeeze my cock dry. I won't do it, am incapable of that kind of intimacy, but if I'd ever risk being someone else, it'd be for her.

"As I was jogging with my head bent low, a sense of someone turning their head and watching overcame me. I clutched my breasts, trying to get them to stop bouncing."

Like the man I wanted to be in the grocery store, I wanted to be that guy in the street. I picture myself standing in an alley wearing my raincoat, eying her from the shadows.

"Finally, though, alone, I made it home. Wet…"

I stroke faster, seeing myself as the hero who would've carried her to safety.

"…breathless…"

Precum dampens my thumb, my hips jutting forward, my dick pulsing in my palm.

"…and in the privacy of my home, at last, I was free to take off everything and protect myself from the cold in a hot bath."

"Christ," I grunt as my orgasm pummels through me and sperm coats my fingers.

I come so hard my chair grates back from the sheer force of it.

She does this to me.

The woman who isn't mine to want.

The woman who is in my dreams, who is mine and mine alone.

My Seraphine.

Made in the USA
Middletown, DE
10 June 2023